NEVER ALONE

Jilly stepped from the gazebo and walked to the canal, not needing the flashlight any-more since the clouds had turned milky gray. She knelt down. The water was calm enough for her to see the shadow of her own reflection.

Then a growing sense that someone was standing behind her cut short her daydream, snapping her back to attention. Just as the image of a person's head began to appear over hers in the still water, an acorn from the oak tree plopped into the canal, sending ripples of waves across the picture.

Jilly leaped to her feet and spun around.

No one was there.

Other Avon Flare Books by
Dian Curtis Regan

GAME OF SURVIVAL
I'VE GOT YOUR NUMBER
THE PERFECT AGE

Jilly's Ghost

Dian Curtis Regan

Dian Curtis Regan

AN AVON FLARE BOOK

AVON BOOKS
A division of
The Hearst Corporation
105 Madison Avenue
New York, New York 10016

Copyright © 1990 by Dian Curtis Regan
Published by arrangment with the author.
Library of Congress Catalog Card Number: 89-91876
ISBN: 0-380-75831-8

First Avon Flare Printing: October 1990

AVON TRADEMARK REG. U.S. PAT. OFF. AND IN OTHER COUNTRIES, MARCA
REGISTRADA, HECHO EN CANADA

Printed in Canada

UNV   10   9   8   7   6   5   4   3   2

For John and Alice Regan, with love

CHAPTER 1

Jilly Milford raced her best friend, Amanda Parks, to the top of the curved staircase. They burst into Jilly's bedroom, dumping their book bags onto the bed.

"I can't believe Kevin Dobbins didn't speak to me today." Amanda caught her breath as she sprawled across the patchwork bedspread.

Jilly offered a sympathetic smile, wishing she had the same kind of problems as her friend. If Kevin Dobbins hadn't spoken to Amanda today, surely a million other guys had. She was hard to miss, even in a crowd, with her tiny waist and delicate features.

Kicking off low heels, Jilly wiggled out of her panty hose, glad to be rid of them on this unusually warm November afternoon. She pulled on her favorite pair of jeans and stretched out on the braided rug beside her bed.

"I mean," Amanda continued, raising herself on one elbow, "we saw each other every night during Thanksgiving break. And now, first day back at school, he acts as if he doesn't even know me."

"You saw him *every* night?" Jilly wondered what two people of the opposite sex could possibly find to talk about for five nights in a row.

"Yeah, he even said 'I love you.' "

"He did?" Jilly came to her knees. "He told you he *loved* you?" Chill bumps crawled up her spine at the thought.

Amanda scrunched a handful of blond hair. "Yes, it was so romantic. Last night we were at the Massapequa

Shopping Center, sitting on the brick wall in the alley behind 7-Eleven—next to the dumpsters.''

She shot a glance at Jilly. ''Well, that wasn't the romantic part.'' Amanda leaned over the edge of the bed so they were face to face. ''He took my hand in his, kissed me, then said, 'Amanda Parks, I love you.' ''

''He called you by your full name?''

''Yes, it was very formal.''

''And he *kissed* you?'' Jilly's face was inches from Amanda's, watching her eyes. Was it true?

''He kissed me days ago.''

''He did?'' Jilly jerked away in surprise. ''Why didn't you tell me?''

''You were in Pennsylvania.''

''There are telephone lines between Pennsylvania and New York.''

Amanda rolled onto her back. ''My mom would kill me if I made a long-distance call unless it was an absolute emergency.''

''Kissing Kevin Dobbins isn't an absolute emergency?''

''Well, to me it is, but I doubt it is to my mom.''

Jilly sat on the edge of the bed, trying to scrunch a handful of her own auburn hair, but it was too short and straight to scrunch. She felt hurt that her best friend had been kissed for the first time and she hadn't been there to share the experience with her—however vicariously.

She peered at Amanda as if her friend should somehow look different now. The words *I've been kissed* should be tattooed across her forehead in Day-Glo colors. Amanda seemed so nonchalant about the whole thing, as though guys kissed her every day of the week.

It made Jilly feel exasperated. She also felt left out.

Amanda sat up. ''I didn't mean to hurt your feelings or make you feel left out.''

Funny how best friends can read your mind.

''The first time it happened,'' Amanda continued, straightening the bedspread, ''I was almost mad at you

2

for not being here to give me moral support. I wasn't sure I'd done it right.''

She blinked her doll eyes, lined in smoky blue. ''I forgot all the things we discussed about keeping your eyes closed, letting the guy kiss you first, and all that.''

Jilly covered her mouth with both hands to keep from laughing.

''It's not funny, Jil. I mean, are you supposed to close your eyes when you *think* he's going to kiss you, or when he gets real close? Or do you wait until he's actually made contact with your lips?''

Amanda was acting out the story as she told it, using the palm of her hand as Kevin's lips. ''What if you close your eyes and he *doesn't* kiss you? He'd think you were weird.''

Jilly gave in to laughter, sliding off the bed onto the braided rug.

Amanda waited with crossed arms for Jilly to get serious. ''You wouldn't have known what to do, either. You're just jealous.''

''You're right.'' She grabbed a tissue from the nightstand to blot her eyes. ''But I have this mental image of you sitting next to Kevin with your eyes closed. Maybe he thought you were asleep, so he kissed you to wake you up. Like Sleeping Beauty and Prince Charming.''

''Cute, Jilly.'' Amanda slid to the floor next to her. ''I've been dying to get you alone all day so I could tell you, and now you're turning it into a big joke. Do you want to hear what happened or not?''

Jilly's curiosity overflowed, like the canal that angled through the Milford's backyard when it poured rain. ''Of course.'' Grinning, she raised her eyebrows a couple times to camouflage the jealousy enveloping her.

Amanda's eyes told her she'd soon burst if she didn't share the details. ''The first night of break, I was outside, sweeping leaves off the porch. Kevin rode up on his bike and we talked until I had to go in. Thursday

3

and Friday, we went for walks, and he held my hand both nights. Then Saturday we walked to the alley behind 7-Eleven. That's where he kissed me. And I already told you what he said to me last night.''

''That's fantastic.''

''No, it's not.''

''How can you say that?''

''It was fantastic when it happened, but today at school I ran into Kevin four times and he didn't even say hello.''

''Maybe he's so overcome with lovesickness he can't speak.''

''It's not funny, Jil, he wouldn't even look at me. What'd I do wrong?''

''Maybe you're not a good kisser.''

''Argggh!'' Amanda ripped a pillow from under the bedspread and attempted to smother Jilly. ''Why'd you have to say that?''

Dodging, Jilly grabbed the attacking pillow. ''Do you want me to ask Kevin if he likes the way you kiss?''

''Stop it. You're giving me a complex. Now I'll be self-conscious the next time he kisses me—if there *is* a next time.''

Amanda folded her long legs. ''Do you suppose that's the reason he's not speaking to me now? Do you think I'm a terrible kisser?''

''I don't know. I've never kissed you.''

Amanda gave her The Look. She moved to the window and hooked her fingers under the bottom edge, giving it a hefty tug to widen the crack. Warm fall breezes whooshed into the room. ''I'll go to my grave wondering what I did to make Kevin Dobbins stop loving me.''

''Maybe you can get your name into *The Guinness Book of World Records* for having the shortest love affair.'' Jilly knew she was being mean, but it seemed that Amanda had more than her share of potential boyfriends lined up for their sophomore year.

Amanda ignored her.

4

Jonathan Nichols rambled across Jilly's mind. It would probably take the entire year to get Jonathan even to notice her.

"Speaking of graves," Amanda said, gazing out the window. "Do you think Mr. McGregor missed you while you were in Pennsylvania?"

"Well, if he's truly supernatural, he'd know I go there every Thanksgiving." Jilly stifled the thought that she'd spent the holiday weekend getting smothered by relatives while Amanda had spent her holiday getting kissed.

"Did you see him last night?"

"No. The moon was full." Jilly moved to the window, remembering the silky moonbeams filtering through her sheer curtains last night, making bright designs on the hardwood floor. "I usually see him when there's no moon, or when it's cloudy. That's when Mr. McGregor turns on the light in the toolshed."

"You know what I was thinking today during Journalism?" Amanda faced her, blue eyes shooting out sparks of enthusiasm. "You'd get a definite *A* if you wrote an article on how this lonely pilgrim died in your backyard and haunts your tool—"

"Wait, wait, wait." Jilly waved her hand for silence the way Mr. Kortman, their Journalism teacher did. "Did you say *pilgrim?*"

"Yeah, he probably came over on the *Mayflower.*"

Jilly knelt on the padded window seat next to Amanda. "Mr. McGregor isn't a Pilgrim. His clothes look like those worn in old movies, maybe from the forties or fifties." She glanced sideways at Amanda. "And I'm *not* going to write about him because he's *my* secret."

Jilly held her friend's gaze for a few moments to show her she meant it. "Besides," she added, "he doesn't haunt the toolshed."

"Okay, the gazebo."

"He doesn't haunt the gazebo either."

"What do you call it when someone who's not alive

anymore appears in the same place over and over? You call it haunting.''

"Well, the word *haunting* sounds scary. There's nothing scary about Mr. McGregor.''

Amanda raised one eyebrow. "How long have you seen this apparition?''

"All my life. You know that.'' Jilly imitated Amanda's crooked eyebrow. "You know I grew up with him living in my backyard.''

"How many times have you spoken with him?''

"Zillions of times.''

"You have?''

"Oh, you mean with him answering back?''

"Yeah, I mean with him answering back.''

"Never.''

"And you totally believe he exists?''

"Of course.''

Amanda circled one finger around her ear in a crazy sign. "Now *that's* scary.'' She moved from the window, scooping her book bag from the bed.

"You believe in him, too,'' Jilly said, feeling defensive. "You're just getting even since I told you Kevin Dobbins stopped loving you because you're a terrible kisser.''

"Oh, Jilly, don't be so *juvenile.* '' Amanda thrust one shoulder forward and scrunched her hair.

Jilly threw a paperback at her.

Ducking out the door, she laughed. "Please cross your fingers that he'll speak to me tomorrow.''

"Who? Mr. McGregor?''

"No, idiot. Kevin Dobbins.'' Amanda clunked down the stairs and out the front door.

Jilly turned back to the window, studying the yard below. She'd decided long ago to keep Mr. McGregor a secret from everyone except Amanda for fear people would think she *was* crazy. But, during her fifteen years in this bedroom, she'd been awakened hundreds of times at odd hours of the night, usually by a train arriving or departing the nearby stop on the Long Island Railroad.

She'd climb out of bed and sit on the window seat to wait for the white-haired man who often appeared through the window of the toolshed, arranging and rearranging rakes and shovels. Sometimes he turned on the light, and sometimes he stayed in the dark, pacing to the canal, the gazebo, then back to the toolshed.

Most of the time his image was smudged and shadowy, but on many nights he looked solid, like a real person. Occasionally Jilly could hear him but not see him, yet she always sensed when he was there.

Jilly had named him Mr. McGregor because her favorite story the first time she saw the ghost was *Peter Rabbit*. The old man reminded her of Farmer McGregor, who'd chased Peter from his vegetable garden.

The ghost reminded her of Grandpa Milford, too. He had lived with them, staying home with Jilly while her parents worked. Through the years, she'd tried to tell him, as well as her parents, about the ghost. Everyone acted interested, even to the extent of following her outside to inspect the shed.

But when they started referring to Mr. McGregor as *Jilly's imaginary playmate,* then as *Jilly's ghost,* she knew she'd never convince them. After Grandpa Milford died, Jilly found comfort in having the old ghost guarding her backyard. She often wondered if he knew she was there.

Suddenly aware of the passage of time, Jilly hurried downstairs to start dinner before her parents got home from work. She wished her Thanksgiving had been as intriguing as Amanda's. As she set the table, she thought about Jonathan Nichols and how great he had looked today at school.

She wondered what it would be like to kiss Jonathan on the brick wall by the dumpsters behind 7-Eleven. She chuckled to herself at the thought. It would probably be more fun to kiss him on the lips.

CHAPTER 2

"We're home!" came Dad's voice from the living room as Jilly clunked ice cubes into three glass mugs.

"Soup's on!" she called back.

Dad came into the kitchen and kissed her cheek as he peeked into the oven. "Looks more like pizza to me."

Jilly groaned at his ancient joke as she watched him wash for dinner in the kitchen sink. He owned a construction company and was always tan from being out of doors. His lean, healthy looks made him resemble a grown-up teenager.

"Where's Mom?" she asked, pouring tea into the mugs. Her parents carpooled to and from work since Mom was office manager of Milford Construction Company.

"Hello, Jil," Mom said, as if on cue, looking fresh at the end of the day in a navy blue dress, her hands full of mail. "Doesn't look good," she said, dropping the mail onto the table and waving the paper.

"What?" Jilly asked. "The pizza?"

"No. This article. The city lost its bid for the computer corporation, which means—"

"No new families will be moving into the area," Dad finished for her in a flat voice.

Jilly knew what that implied. The construction business had been so slow lately her Dad had talked of mov-

8

ing to Florida where, according to him, people were flocking like seagulls.

Jilly ate dinner in silence, listening to her parents' discussion. She couldn't imagine moving away from the big old house on Atwater Place. Not after living here her entire life. She waited for them to ask her opinion about the move, but they never did.

After dinner it was Jilly's turn to take out the garbage. As she dragged the bags to the curb, something in the neighbor's driveway caught her eye. A moped. Royal blue with a decal of a spaceship on the frame.

Jilly's curiosity was stirred. She knew the Sheehans' house had finally sold after standing empty for almost two years—another sign the city wasn't in a growth spurt. The new family must have moved in while she was in Pennsylvania.

But the big question in Jilly's mind was: Who owned the moped? A male or a female? Having a new girl in the neighborhood would be fun. But having a new guy around might be more fun—at least a guy old enough to drive a moped.

Jilly walked a little closer. A space-fighter's sword rested against the front porch. Her curiosity dwindled. Maybe the guy was only eight-years-old if he played with a sword.

Stepping over the low shrubs separating the two houses, she spotted a basketball hoop leaning against the garage door. That was a good sign. Maybe there were two sons: an eight-year-old *and* a teenager.

Suddenly feeling as if she were trespassing, Jilly hopped back over the shrub to her own yard.

"Who goes there?" came a male voice from above her.

Jilly looked up. The Sheehans had built a loft over the garage just before they were transferred out of state. Leaning out the window was a guy about her age, wear-

9

ing some kind of helmet on his head. He was pointing what appeared to be a gun at her.

"It's me. Jilly Milford. Your neighbor." Jilly started to raise her hands in surrender, then stopped. She wasn't doing anything wrong; she was in her own yard. "I was just—"

"Stop," he commanded. "I'll come right down."

Jilly wasn't so sure she wanted him to come right down if he had a gun. Weren't there laws against pointing guns at your neighbors? Even in New York?

In a few seconds the guy came out the front door and strode toward her, gun at his side. The face guard of the helmet was down so she couldn't see his face. Stopping in front of her, he remained quiet, as if he was taking inventory.

Jilly felt self-conscious. What was wrong with him? She was hoping for a guy her age, but not this. Not an alien from another world. The gun, she noted, was a toy ray gun like her young cousins in Pennsylvania owned.

She raised her right hand. "How," she said, lowering her voice an octave. "Me friend." She thought she heard a laugh from under the space helmet.

He pulled off the obnoxious thing. Dark hair was flattened to his head from the shape of the helmet. He was tall, average looking, with the beginnings of a mustache fuzzing his upper lip. A jagged scar sliced across the edge of one eye, making his eyelid sag.

Jilly tried not to look him in the eye for fear he'd think she was staring at his scar. She wondered how it had happened. Maybe he lasered himself with his own ray gun.

He raised his right hand, mimicking her. "How," he returned. "Me Russell. Russell Talley." He stared at her as if he were in a trance. "Where you from?"

"Here." Jilly motioned around her. "Right here. Born and raised. Where you fr—" She cleared her throat, correcting herself. "Where *are* you from?"

He didn't answer. Instead he slowly raised his head until his gaze met the darkening sky.

Jilly followed his gaze. "Up?" she asked. "Up . . . upstate New York!" she exclaimed, feeling proud of her deduction. She'd better get away from this guy. He was a loony tune.

"I think my mom's calling me." She backed toward her house. "Maybe I'll run into you at school sometime."

"Apollo."

"Right. Apollo High School."

He raised his other hand, still holding the ray gun, and touched it to his forehead above the scar, giving her a salute. "Hot jets and a smooth flight."

"Right," she said again. "Same to you."

He looked pleased.

Jilly ran into the house. Russell Talley gave her the royal creeps.

After the kitchen was cleaned and her homework completed, Jilly assembled her books and papers for the next day, then poured a glass of orange juice. Her parents had gone upstairs to watch television. Clicking off the light, she toured the downstairs, shutting curtains and turning off lamps.

This ancient house was as comfortable as a pair of old blue jeans. A feeling of panic rose inside of her at the thought of moving away. She knew she had to leave some day, but as long as it was her choice, it would be all right.

If she had her way, her parents would always live here so she could return any time she wanted. Leaving for any other reason would be too hard.

Jilly ran her hand along the polished wood banister as she followed its curve up the stairway, remembering the times she'd almost killed herself sliding down it on her stomach. And all the Christmas mornings when she couldn't run down the twenty-six steps fast enough.

Entering her room, she curled into her favorite spot on the pillowed window seat to sip her orange juice. Her eyes traveled the room, resting on the tiger oak bureau and dresser her grandfather had built for her when she was a little girl. They belonged in this room with the lattice oak woodwork, the curved ceiling, and the high rounded windows. The furniture would never fit in a modern new house in a Florida suburb.

Leaning her head against the window frame, she watched moon shadows skitter across the backyard, turning wavy as they moved across the water in the canal. Bare branches from the weeping willow tree brushed the ground, as if nature was tidying up in the crisp night breeze.

Shivering, Jilly reached to close the window Amanda had opened earlier. A lone figure moving across the yard caught her eye. "Good evening, Mr. McGregor," she whispered softly to herself. "You might be needing a sweater tonight."

Jilly chuckled at her own comment. Ghosts didn't feel the cold. They didn't feel anything. Mr. McGregor wore the same baggy white shirt with dark pants held up by suspenders, no matter how cold the New York winters got.

Her chuckle caught in her throat as the figure came around the gazebo. In the full moon's light, the person's head was oversized and misshapen.

It was not Mr. McGregor creeping through her backyard tonight. It was Russell Talley.

CHAPTER 3

The next morning at school, Jilly followed Jonathan Nichols down the crowded hallway. Staring at the dark hair curling down the back of his head thrilled her. Maybe if she stared hard enough, he'd turn around and say, "Jilly! There you are. I've been looking for a girl like you all my life. Come walk with me. Be my date for the Winter Carnival."

The last part of the daydream made her toenails tingle. What she wouldn't give to be Jonathan Nichols's date for the Winter Carnival.

"Jilly! There you are."

The voice was not Jonathan's. It was Amanda's. And Amanda's arm was linked through Andy Spinner's.

With reluctance, Jilly stopped tailing Jonathan and watched him disappear around a corner. She sighed, pausing by a water fountain to wait for Amanda and Andy to wind their way through the flow of students.

Jilly wondered how come it was so easy for Amanda to strike up friendships with guys. Why couldn't she have the nerve to link arms with Jonathan and walk with him down the hallway?

Amanda arrived at the water fountain in a rush. Thrusting a handful of papers at Jilly, she winked. A wink between them was a sign something was happening which couldn't be discussed at the present time. "Please hand these in to Mr. Kortman for me."

"Where will you be?" Jilly asked, stuffing the papers

13

into her notebook. Was Amanda crazy? She couldn't cut class without getting caught. Why would she even take the chance?

"I'll be there. A little late. Cover for me?" Amanda gave her a look that meant *Don't ask stupid questions in front of Andy. I'll explain later.*

"Mr. Kortman won't notice if I'm absent since he lets us sit at different tables every day. But if he does, tell him I'm in the girls' room."

Andy was beginning to look bored. Jilly waved them off and hurried on to Journalism as the bell rang.

Jonathan Nichols's table was already surrounded, so Jilly joined another group. Today she'd get to work with the guys who pasted up the sports page. Great. *Those who don't play sports write about those who do.*

Jilly went to work, kicking herself for the unkind thoughts she was having about the guys at her table, Jeff Underdahl and Li Sing Lai. It wasn't their fault they were small and unathletic.

And besides, if she extended the theory to herself, she should be working on the society page—as in: *Those who have no social life write about those who do.*

Jeff and Li Sing were nice, easy to joke with, but unattractive to her. She wondered if attraction was a law of nature. How much attention a guy gave her was inversely proportional to how attractive she thought he was. Guys who made her heart stop seemed to look right through her as though she were invisible. And guys she barely noticed always helped her, called her on the phone, and stopped to talk to her in the hallways.

Maybe there was a formula for attraction: $A/J = GL + GP$. Attraction for Jilly equals good looks plus great personality. And the inverse formula would be $J/A = N + J + W$. Attraction *to* Jilly equals nerds plus jerks plus weirdos.

Funny that Russell Talley should pop into her mind at that precise moment. Jilly wondered how he was far-ing his first week at Apollo High. Surely he'd been smart enough to leave his space helmet and sword at home.

"Jilly, you're pasting the wrong caption under that picture," Li Sing said, grabbing her hand before the glue touched the contact paper.

The picture was a great shot of Apollo High's star fullback spiking the football in the end zone after scoring a winning touchdown. The caption read, "Pride of Apollo, Michelle Rabinowitz, nets tennis championship."

"Sorry," Jilly said.

Li Sing held onto her hand a bit longer than was necessary. Jilly glanced at his embarrassed smile as he let go. His touch didn't affect her at all, but if Jonathan Nichols had grabbed her hand, now that would be a different—

"Thanks, friend." Amanda bumped her shoulder as she sneaked into place, minus Andy Spinner.

"What—?"

"Andy was rounding up a group of kids to pose with the principal for the yearbook." Amanda scrunched a handful of hair.

Jilly wondered why Andy hadn't asked her to pose, too. She'd been standing right there as available as she could be. Obviously he was handpicking kids for the picture and she wasn't a choice.

Jilly forced herself to stop wondering why Amanda always had neat things happening to her. The neatest thing that had happened to Jilly lately was a perfect attendance award for first quarter. Big deal as far as her social life was concerned.

Hello, Jilly? This is Jonathan Nichols. I just heard you won an award for perfect attendance. Wow, I'm so impressed! Will you go out with me now? Maybe we could go to the brick wall behind 7-Eleven next to the dumpsters.

15

Jilly groaned, hanging up her imaginary phone call, and concentrated on the paste-up job in front of her.

Class finished early, since Mr. Kortman wanted time to explain their new assignment. Jilly was proud of the article she'd written for the last issue of the school newspaper, the *Apollo Apogee*, named after the highest point in the universe. The article was about the bell tower the school's alumni were building in the courtyard. The piece, along with a picture she'd taken, had made the front page.

Jilly jotted down their new assignment—a feature article on a local person of interest to the community. Leave it to Mr. Kortman to be so general, forcing them to use their own brains. It'd be a lot easier if he just handed out names of interesting people to interview.

When the lunch bell rang, Amanda followed Jilly out the door. "Well?" she said, stepping into the flow of students.

"Well, what?" Jilly asked, hurrying to keep up with her.

"Are you going to write your article about Mr. McGregor? He'd be perfect. A local person of interest to the community."

"He's dead. How interesting can he be?"

Amanda stopped at her locker. "Mr. Kortman didn't say the person had to be living. Mr. McGregor must have been an interesting person or he wouldn't be a ghost."

"Why do you say that?"

"Because ghosts usually have committed some horrendous crime and are doomed to wander through eternity repenting it." Amanda struggled to fit her armload of books onto the top shelf of the locker.

Jilly couldn't imagine Mr. McGregor committing any horrendous crime. "Where did you learn that?"

"I read it somewhere. Not everyone becomes a ghost

after they die. Only people who leave something in their life unresolved.''

"I'm not sure I believe that. Anyway, I have no idea who Mr. McGregor really is, so there's no way of researching him.''

Amanda freshened her lip gloss in the tiny mirror taped to the back of her locker door. ''The courthouse keeps legal documents dating back for years. You can look up the name of every person who's lived in your house since it was built.''

She slammed the door and twirled the combination dial. A few steps down the hall, they stopped at Jilly's locker.

"After you find out the people's names,'' Amanda continued, ''you can look up old newspapers at the library to see if any violent crimes were committed in your house.''

Jilly was interested in spite of herself, but the idea of someone being murdered in her own home turned her blood to ice.

"Do it.'' Amanda slammed Jilly's locker as if to punctuate her command.

"Let's go to lunch.'' Jilly took long strides down the hallway, hoping to change the subject.

"If you don't write about Mr. McGregor, I will.''

That stopped her. Grabbing Amanda's wrist, she pulled her out of the crowd, backing her against the wall. The same feeling of panic that had stirred Jilly earlier over the possibility of moving to Florida overwhelmed her once more at the unpleasant prospect of learning the truth about her ghost—and exposing him to the world, via the *Apollo Apogee*.

"Amanda Parks, are you my best friend?''

Amanda pressed her lips together as if it was a dumb question.

"Have we always kept each other's secrets?''

"Yes.''

17

"Have we—?"

"You're not a little kid anymore." Amanda twisted her arm away from Jilly's frantic grasp. "Mr. McGregor is *not* your grandfather's ghost sent back to earth to watch over you."

Amanda's tone was close to mocking. It made Jilly sorry she'd confided something so personal, even to her best friend.

Cocking her head, Amanda now looked apologetic at being so flip about such a sensitive issue. "Jilly, it's time you grew up and stopped considering Mr. McGregor your own personal ghost. *Jilly's ghost,* as your mom calls him. It's time you told others about him. The people of Massapequa have a right to know about something this unusual happening in their community."

Jilly didn't answer. Her friend's words hurt her ears as much as the buzzing lunch bell under which she was standing.

Amanda refused to give up. "Maybe the nicest thing you could do for Mr. McGregor is to call in an expert on poltergeists and let them do whatever it is they do to put spirits to rest."

Part of Jilly believed Amanda was right. Another part of her refused to listen. "Are you through lecturing?"

Amanda waved at a group of guys who were hooting at her as they passed. Jilly felt a twinge that none of the hoots were aimed at her, but she didn't know anyone in the group who found her hootable.

"First of all," Jilly began in her defense, "I know Mr. McGregor is not my grandfather's ghost. He was appearing in my backyard long before my grandfather died. It was just a stage I went through in the sixth grade when I really missed my grandpa and wanted to believe it might be him out there, guarding my bedroom window."

Jilly felt embarrassed now, saying it out loud.

"Second, I've never investigated the ghost because

18

I like him just the way he is. If I research all this, and he turns out to be the Massapequa strangler of 1950, I'll be sorry I found out. I don't want to know who he is. I mean, *was*."

Jilly felt cornered, even though Amanda already knew almost everything about her. "I've made up stuff about Mr. McGregor all my life, and I like *my* version of his story better than anything truth could bring to it."

Amanda's eyes doubled in size. "What kind of stuff?" She looked as if Jilly was about to tell her the secret of the century.

Jilly had never told anyone the stories she'd day-dreamed about the ghost's life. Some of the stories she'd even written down. But it was too personal to share—even with Amanda.

"Never mind." Jilly was sorry she'd brought it up.

Amanda grabbed her shoulder. "Tell me."

Sighing, Jilly stared at the ceiling. Which story would appease her?"

"Come on, Jil." Amanda had the patience of a two-year-old.

"Okay, okay." Jilly turned sideways and leaned her forehead against the concrete wall. "This is so embarrassing." She glanced sideways at Amanda, hoping she'd lost her attention.

She hadn't.

"Okay," she said again. "Pretend Mr. McGregor had a grandson."

"And?"

"And one day I meet him, and it turns out we're the same age."

"And?"

"And his name is Craig. Craig McGregor."

"Why Craig?"

"I don't know. I just like the name Craig." Jilly was starting to squirm against the wall, feeling pinned under

19

her friend's hand. Why was Amanda making her tell her deepest secrets right here in the cafeteria hallway?

"And?"

"What do you mean—and? That's it. One of the stories I made up."

"Tell me another."

"No!" Jilly felt exasperated. "The point I'm trying to make, Amanda Parks, is that Mr. McGregor is *my* secret and you have to respect that as my friend. If word leaked out about him, every TV station in New York would descend on my backyard and set up cameras to film the alleged apparition."

And, Jilly added to herself, Mr. McGregor wouldn't like it. *He'd never forgive me for not keeping him a secret; I just know it.*

"Okay, you win." Amanda stepped back, giving Jilly breathing space. "Neither one of us will write what would probably be the best news story of all time for the *Apogee.*"

Disappointment touched Amanda's eyes. "I might even have been nominated for the Pulitzer Prize in high school journalism."

"Hey, I think I see Kevin Dobbins," Jilly said, trying anything to get Amanda off the subject of exploiting her life's secret.

"Where? Where?" Amanda scrunched her hair in double-time as her eyes flitted over the cafeteria crowd.

Jilly knew it was a mean trick, but she was starving. "Come on. Lunch will be over before we get through the line."

For once Amanda didn't argue. As they headed into the cafeteria, Jilly felt relieved she hadn't had to answer the last of Amanda's questions—the one about why she'd never called in an expert to put Mr. McGregor's spirit to rest.

She believed those kind of things were possible. But she didn't *want* Mr. McGregor to disappear. He'd been as much a part of her childhood as the worn, stuffed kitten named Pokie that she'd had since she was born. She liked things just the way they were.

Why did everyone want her to change all of a sudden? Move her to Florida? Expose her lifelong friend—even though he was dead? And make her put up with a new, weird neighbor?

The icy feeling shivered through her blood again as she recalled the sight of Russell Talley sneaking around her backyard last night. Had he seen Mr. McGregor? Had he zapped the ghost with his ray gun?

The ridiculous image of Russell Talley in his space helmet tripping through her backyard in the dark, blasting a dead person with laser rays, made her laugh in spite of how angry Russell's nosiness made her feel.

Why couldn't everyone, including Amanda, back off and leave her alone? Why couldn't her life keep running along, boring and predictable the way it always had before? At least then she knew what to expect.

Part of her longed for the excitement of a change, yet another part of her sensed a coming danger.

CHAPTER 4

Jilly licked a stamp and pounded it onto the annual thank-you card addressed to her Pennsylvania relatives. Grabbing a jacket, she raced upstairs to the TV room where her parents were watching television.

"I'm going out to mail this," she said, waving the card.

"Can I drive you?" her mom asked, looking up. "I don't like you going out alone after dark."

"Mom, I'm just going to the corner. I'll be back in two seconds." Jilly paused, feeling mischievous. "Unless you let *me* take the car. Then I'll be back in two hours."

Her parents laughed. She still had two years to go before she was old enough to get her driver's license, but she couldn't wait.

"Just be careful," her mom called after her, "and don't talk to strangers."

Jilly was down the stairs and out the front door before Mom could change her mind. Parents must have to memorize a list of clichés before they're allowed to have kids, she thought, walking fast to keep warm. Like, *"Don't talk to strangers", "Be home by midnight", "Better take a sweater",* and *"Finish what's on your plate."*

A noise behind her she normally would have ignored now made her jump, all because of her mother's warnings.

Jilly whipped around. It was only some kid riding up the street on a moped. No big deal.

Jilly looked again. The kid seemed to have a head too large for his body. He hopped the curb, swerved to keep from hitting a tree, then stopped a few feet ahead of her, cutting the engine.

"Hello, Russell," Jilly said in a flat tone, wondering why Jonathan Nichols couldn't be riding through her neighborhood tonight instead of Russell Talley.

The face guard on Russell's space helmet was up so he could see in the dark. The glow from a street light emphasized his scrawny body and giant head, making Jilly cough to keep from laughing at the sight of him.

"What's the password?" Russell's monotone voice sounded computer-generated. He blocked Jilly's path with his moped and an outstretched arm.

Was he joking? She couldn't tell.

"Sauerkraut." The word had been the first to pop into her head since that's what her mom had served for dinner tonight.

"Negative."

Somehow she wasn't surprised. She doubted the word was *bratwurst* either, even though that's what Mom had served with the sauerkraut.

Jilly felt impatient with Russell blocking her way and playing his childish games. "Why can't you say *no* instead of *negative* like *normal* people?"

He ignored her comment. "Repeat request. What is the password?"

Annoyance bristled inside her. Mom had said not to talk to strangers. Did that include strange people, too?

"The password is . . . get out of my way or I'll knock your space helmet all the way to New Jersey."

Russell pulled off his helmet. Was he afraid she'd really deck him?

"You're cute when you're mad."

"Jeez!" Jilly spun around, turning her back to him.

23

He finally said something *normal,* and it had to be something which embarrassed her more than his weirdness.

"We need to work together on this."

What was he talking about now? She faced him. "We need to work together on *what?*"

"On the problem in your backyard."

Jilly's heart skittered. "Problem?"

"You mean you haven't noticed?" He got off the moped, adjusted the kickstand, and stepped toward her.

Jilly backed away, holding out the thank-you card as a shield.

"There's something strange going on in your backyard."

"No, there's not." She blurted out the words so abruptly, even *she* could hear the doubt in her own voice. Certainly he'd heard it, too.

His eyes glinted wickedly in the street light. The jagged scar traced an eerie shadow across one side of his face.

For a moment Jilly was afraid of him. She could almost see the wheels turning inside his head—making plans to trap and expose Mr. McGregor.

"You said you've lived here all your life," Russell persisted. "You must know he appears, what he does, who he is. Tell me about him."

"About *who?*" Jilly knew exactly *who,* but somehow she had to throw Russell off. Was he the only one besides her who had seen the ghost? If so, she'd have to make him think it was his own imagination.

He narrowed his eyes at her. "You can't be that stupid."

"Excuse me." Jilly stepped around him, moving ahead at a brisk pace. She didn't have to stand there and be insulted.

"Hey," Russell called, running after her. He caught

24

her arm, making her drop the thank-you card. "I didn't mean that. I'm sorry."

Russell scooped the envelope from the sidewalk, dusted it off on his jeans, and handed it to her. "I just thought if we worked together, we could blow this thing wide open."

"Blow what thing wide open?" Jilly jerked her arm away, vowing silently to Mr. McGregor she'd do anything to keep this maniac away from him.

"Well, just think about it." Russell pulled his helmet on, leaving the face guard up. "We can talk later." He saluted her as usual—two fingers touching the scar beside his eye.

Returning to his moped, he swung a leg over the frame as if he were mounting a horse, nudged up the kickstand, then bounced off the curb, swerving down the dark street. He called back over his shoulder, "Zero gravity and warp speed!"

The next day during lunch, Jilly watched the cafeteria helper spoon Irish stew onto her plate. She wished it looked as appetizing as it smelled. Handing money to the cashier, she followed Amanda to their regular table in the sophomore section of the cafeteria.

"So," Amanda began, settling into place. "Who are you going to interview for your *Apogee* article?"

Jilly could tell by her friend's expression that she was hoping to hear: "You were absolutely right, Amanda. I'm doing my article on Mr. McGregor." But after last night's episode with Russell Talley, Jilly was even more determined not to write about her ghost.

"I'm not sure who to interview." She blew on a spoonful of stew, wishing she could dump it and go out for a burger. "I thought about talking to my grandparents, but then I heard everyone else has the same idea. Who are you interviewing?"

Amanda gave her a funny look. "My grandparents."

"Oops. Sorry." Foot in mouth, Jilly said to herself.

"It'll be easy since they're moving here."

"Did they find an apartment?"

"No, they can't afford one on Long Island, but they've put their house up for sale, and are determined to live near their grandkids. Mom wants them to live with us, but we don't have enough room, so Plan B is to build an addition onto our house with the money they make from selling their home."

"That's a great idea." Amanda's mom was divorced, so it was just her, Amanda, and a little sister, Hollianne.

"Yeah, but Mom doesn't know where to begin, who to call, how much is reasonable to pay, and all that."

"How about calling Milford Construction Company?"

"Oh, she'd planned to call your dad and ask him to recommend someone who does remodeling. Your parents build only new houses, don't they?"

"Well, business is slow. I think they'll take whatever work they can get." Jilly hadn't told Amanda about the impending move to Florida. She was saving the bad news as long as possible.

Amanda smiled at her. "I'll tell my mom. I think her first concern is about hiring an architect to design the addition."

"Milford Construction Company comes complete with an architect-in-training."

"It does?"

"Yeah, my mom. She's taking classes two nights a week at Stony Brook. It'll be a while before she gets her degree, but I'm sure she'd love to work with your mom since they've known each other forever."

Amanda took three tiny bites in a row. "Wouldn't it be great if your parents took the job? They'd be at my house every day, so you and I could go home and study together."

And, Jilly added to herself, maybe she and Amanda

26

could stretch out the job as long as possible to make her parents forget about Florida for a while.

"Look!" Amanda almost choked on her stew.

Jilly's eyes followed her gaze. Kevin Dobbins was walking Traci Wooster to another table. He glanced up as he started to sit next to Traci, paused, then moved to the other side of the table so his back was to them.

"Did you see that?" Amanda hissed. "He saw us, then he moved so he wasn't facing me."

Jilly wasn't sure if Kevin actually looked at them or if he merely preferred the other side of the table. "Relax, Amanda, he just wanted to sit across from Traci so he could stare into her sexy blue eyes."

Amanda flinched, giving her a wounded look. "What's wrong with *my* sexy blue eyes?"

"Nothing." Jilly took a last bite of stew. "Maybe her blue eyes know when to close when Kevin kisses her."

The instant the words were out of her mouth, Jilly knew it was a tacky thing to say. She sensed Amanda stiffening beside her.

Dropping her fork, Amanda jerked to her feet to dump her lunch tray.

Jilly smiled up at her, but her friend still looked hurt.

"See you in study hall," Amanda said in a clipped voice, leaving in a rush.

Jilly finished her milk, feeling awful all of a sudden. Why hadn't she jumped to apologize to her friend? Was she so jealous that she enjoyed seeing Amanda hurt?

That's ridiculous, she thought, cutting into the piece of chocolate pie in front of her. She stared at the pie, suddenly losing her taste for her favorite dessert. How could she enjoy it after being so nasty to her best friend?

Jilly dumped her lunch tray, complete with the uneaten pie. Giving up dessert made her feel duly punished for her snide remark. She only hoped Amanda would forgive her.

27

CHAPTER 5

With bowed head, Jilly studied the tips of her shoes as she walked to study hall, still feeling angry at herself for the stupid comment she'd made to Amanda.

"Hold this, will ya?"

Her head snapped up as she recognized the voice. Jonathan Nichols was standing outside the door to study hall, juggling books, a jacket, and a camera.

He was holding the camera out to her.

Jilly balanced her books in one arm and grabbed the camera, telling herself Jonathan hadn't been standing there waiting just for her—Jilly Alice Milford. She simply happened to be the first person with a free hand who'd come down the hall when he needed help.

Jonathan dropped his books to the floor, struggled into his jacket, then reached for the camera. "Mr. Kortman got permission for me to use study hall time to photograph the person I'm interviewing for the *Apogee*," he explained.

"Oh." Jilly wondered if she had enough nerve to ask if he needed an assistant. "Who are you interviewing?" she asked instead.

"Mrs. Dancy. Over at Dancy's Diner. She's a friend of my grandmother's. That's how I found out she started selling pies during the sixties, and now runs the most popular diner in town."

"Oh." Say something more intelligent than *Oh*, Jilly thought, scolding herself.

28

Jonathan grabbed the camera, slipping the strap around his neck. "Who are you interviewing?"

"Um." *Great, Jilly. Um is way more intelligent than Oh.* "Mrs. Dancy," she answered, grinning.

"What?" He stopped abruptly and frowned at her.

"I'm kidding," Jilly said.

Jonathan didn't laugh, but he did look relieved.

So much for the humor approach.

Jonathan scooped his books from the floor. "Thanks" was all he said.

"Oh, um." *That's better, Jilly. Put the two words together.*

He stopped. "Yeah?"

She sighed. What did she have to lose? "Do you need any more help?" She hoped she didn't sound desperate.

"No."

Well that was certainly easy and painless, as far as rejections go.

"Oh, I get it," he continued. "You mean—can you go with me?"

Jilly nodded. *What did he need? An engraved invitation?*

He laughed.

Great. He doesn't laugh at my joke, then he laughs when I try to be serious.

"Now, now, Milford. Are you trying to get out of study hall?" He laughed again.

"No, I—"

"Shame on you." He waved a finger at her. "Don't get too bored, now, while I'm at Dancy's Diner eating some of her great chocolate pudding cake. Guess you could call this a real piece-of-cake assignment." He chuckled.

Jonathan took off down the hallway before she could decide whether or not to laugh—or to defend herself.

How does Amanda do it? Jilly wondered, stepping into the classroom. She let her books fall with a loud smack at the only empty desk. Amanda was sitting in the front of the room. Usually they saved each other a place. Amanda must still be mad.

Later that night, after dinner, Jilly took out the garbage as fast as she could. She didn't want to run into Russell Talley again and have to answer more questions. Besides she had an appointment right now for her own interview for Journalism.

The only good that had come from her brief encounter with Jonathan Nichols was that it'd given her an idea of someone to interview. Her dad had started his own business the same as Mrs. Dancy had. Milford Construction Company hadn't been around since the sixties, but still, Dad was an important person in the community—an entrepreneur who built beautiful homes.

Jilly raced upstairs to grab her notebook and pencil, then bounded down the steps to the family room. Mr. Kortman said it was important not to be late for your interview.

Dad was lending her his tape recorder, just in case she didn't get everything written down. He set it up and turned it on.

The interview was a breeze. Jilly barely had to ask questions because Dad was eager to tell her all about his career. And Mom was there to make corrections when he got the dates wrong or exaggerated too much.

This is a piece-of-cake assignment, too, Jilly thought later as she typed it up in her room. She decided to leave out the negative part about having to move away due to the slowdown of business, and end the story with an anecdote about the addition her mom and dad might be designing for Amanda's grandparents. Mr. Kortman liked them to use lots of anecdotes, especially ones with human interest.

It was late by the time Jilly finished the rough draft of her article. She assembled her books for morning, then slipped into bed wearing a pajama top over her sweats because she was too tired to finish changing into her pajamas.

An hour or so later, the rumbling of the train in the distance woke her from a light sleep. Jilly got out of bed to close the window. The night air had turned frigid. Curling onto the window seat, she studied the dark backyard as she had a zillion times before, waiting to see if there was any movement tonight.

There was. Near the gazebo. The untrained eye might never notice a faint whitish form moving between the gazebo and the canal. The image wasn't very sharp tonight. Only she knew what to look for.

Jilly rose to her knees, leaning her forehead against the cold glass as she gazed toward the canal. "Mr. McGregor, please don't worry." The whispered words were meant to comfort herself more than him. "You can trust me. I'll never tell them about you; I promise."

The form was hidden among the trees now. Still, Jilly knew he was pacing, pacing, as he always did. He never sat in the gazebo, but moved constantly. He was a restless spirit.

A sudden noise disturbed the night. Jilly jumped, immediately thinking of Russell. But it was only a couple of alley cats having a loud disagreement somewhere in the night.

Jilly pushed a tiny button on her watch to light the numbers. 1:15 A.M. She hoped Russell was sound asleep right now.

An idea struck her. Was there any way to warn Mr. McGregor about Russell? Jilly considered the thought, then dismissed it as ridiculous. First of all, nothing can be a threat to a person who's already dead. Second of all, she'd never tried to communicate with Mr. McGregor.

Why not? she asked herself. Was she afraid she'd scare

31

him away? Or was she afraid *he'd* scare *her* away? After all, he's a ghost, isn't he?

Amanda's words came back to her. What if Mr. McGregor had committed some horrendous crime? What if he really was—or used to be—an evil person? Would he appear to her if she stayed in the backyard some night? Would he threaten her?

Jilly's eyes squinted at the yard until the movement caught her eye again. Now he was heading toward the tool shed. It didn't matter that the door was padlocked. He still went inside. Right through the wall, she assumed.

Maybe finding out more about Mr. McGregor was not such a bad idea after all. It might help save him, instead of hurt him.

Besides, her days in the Atwater house were numbered. She didn't have much time if she wanted to discover the ghost's true identity. And she had to admit, Amanda's theories made her curious.

Jilly stood, shivering, then headed back for the warmth beneath her bedcovers as she finalized the plan in her mind. If Russell Talley was sneaking around her backyard searching for clues about the ghost, she would beat him to any clues that might exist.

And she would start first thing in the morning.

CHAPTER 6

Jilly released the latch on the back door, hoping it wouldn't click loudly enough to wake her mom and dad. Shivering in the frosty morning darkness, she switched on a flashlight to guide her way down the steps and into the backyard.

Not knowing exactly what she was looking for, Jilly toured the yard, tracing the steps she'd watched Mr. McGregor travel year after year.

Funny how she'd played in this backyard countless times when she was a little girl, always with the knowledge of Mr. McGregor's illusive presence, yet without fear. Knowing he was *around* gave her the same comfortable feeling she'd had years ago when her grandfather sat on the back porch swing, reading and "keeping an eye on her so she didn't slip into the canal," as he used to say.

But now that she was in the yard hoping to discover some clues about the identity of the ghost, that comforting feeling was gone. An eeriness trailed her as she paced from the gazebo to the canal, from the canal to the toolshed, then back to the gazebo. An eeriness that raised the small hairs on the back of her neck.

What was she looking for? She wasn't sure. How would she know a clue if she found one?

Stopping in the gazebo, Jilly played the flashlight along the railing, the roof, and the wooden love seat. It was all so familiar to her, especially the flat top of the railing where, years ago, she'd carved her own initials into the wood with a screwdriver from the toolshed. J.A.M. Every summer on her birthday she'd added the year, until there was a long list of them—and until her dad had caught her. He hadn't been too happy about it so she'd stopped, somewhere in the middle of the eighties.

Jilly had gotten the idea of carving her initials because someone else had carved the railings before her. Tiny hearts, barely touching, like this: ♋

Whoever had done it had carved the hearts in other places, too—inside the toolshed, on the front porch, and even on the windowsill in her bedroom. She liked to believe it'd been another teenage girl, like herself, who'd lived in this house a long, long time ago and had slept in her room.

A sudden noise made her jump. She clicked off the flashlight and listened until she heard it again. A whirring sound met her ears. After listening for a few moments, she realized the sounds were coming from the front of the house where the paper boy was tossing newspapers onto porches from his ten-speed.

Relieved, Jilly stepped from the gazebo and walked to the canal, not needing the flashlight anymore since clouds were turning milky gray from the first rays of the sun.

Kneeling on the bank of the canal, she peered into the brown water, wondering exactly what she was looking for. The water was calm enough for her to see the shadow of her own reflection. Her tousled hair reminded her she needed to leave plenty of time this morning to get ready for school. This was the day her Journalism class called on businesses to buy advertising for the *Apogee*. Mr. Kortman required them to dress up and look their best since they were representing Apollo High to the community.

Jilly thought about Jonathan Nichols as she gazed into

34

the canal. Maybe she could find a way to ask him about his interview with Mrs. Dancy. Then he might ask about her interview, and bingo, they'd be having a real conversation.

A growing sense that someone was standing behind her snapped Jilly back to attention. Just as the image of a person's head began to appear over hers in the still water, an acorn from the overhanging oak tree plopped into the canal, sending ripples of waves across the picture.

Jilly leaped to her feet and spun around.

No one was there.

The hairs on the back of her neck stood on end once more as she bolted for the house. Any second she expected invisible hands to grab her from behind.

The door opened as Jilly dashed toward it.

She took the steps in one leap, landing inside the kitchen.

"Well, good morning." Her dad leaned out the door as if he were looking for whoever had chased his daughter into the house. "You look as though you've seen a ghost." He started to laugh, then stopped.

Jilly knew she must have a terrified look on her face.

"Are you all right?" he asked.

She nodded, backing into the kitchen.

"Where've you been?" Worry flickered in his eyes.

"Nowhere." Jilly tried to calm her breathing as she slipped off her jacket and slung it over a chair. She now felt silly at her reaction to nothing. "Just out in the backyard."

He closed the door, cocking his head at her. "What were you doing out at this hour?"

Jilly poured a mug full of milk and put it into the microwave for hot chocolate. "Um, watching the sunrise." She hoped he believed her since she was usually the last one to drag out of bed in the morning.

"Alone?"

35

"Dad!" Jilly laughed at his raised eyebrows. "You thought I was having a rendezvous? Like this?" She still wore her pajama top over a pair of sweats, socks, and bedroom slippers.

He laughed, as if he'd just noticed what she was wearing. "I'm kidding, Jil. Go get ready and we'll drop you off at school. Your mom needs to go in early this morning to work on her new project."

Jilly set the cup of steaming milk on the table and spooned in a generous helping of chocolate. "What new project?"

"I thought you knew. She's designing an add-on apartment for the Parkses' house so Amanda's grandparents can move in but not actually live with them."

"You took the job for Amanda's mom!" Jilly grinned at her dad as she licked chocolate off the spoon.

"A job is a job."

"Terrific!"

He scooped a Danish onto a plate and handed it to her. "Go get dressed or we'll all be late."

Jilly hurried up the steps, balancing the plate on top of the mug of hot chocolate. Her excitement over Dad's news overruled her jitters from this morning's fright.

And, as far as her disappointing backyard search went, the clues she didn't find this morning, she'd look for later—preferably in the unscary light of midday.

CHAPTER 7

Jilly caught sight of Amanda leaning against Andy Spinner's locker before homeroom. Next to Andy Spinner.

Her plan to celebrate with Amanda over their parents' partnership would have to wait. Jilly couldn't carry on a normal conversation with her best friend in front of Andy. He always stared at her without saying anything, and addressed all his comments to Amanda. How could her friend talk to him anyway? He was an ice cube.

Jilly laughed when she saw how Amanda was dressed. She was wearing the same outfit as Jilly. At the mall one day, they'd both gone crazy over a jean dress, and had promised each other they'd never wear it on the same day. And they wouldn't have if they'd talked on the phone last night like they normally did.

Okay, Jilly said to herself, *it's my fault for making Amanda mad at me. I'll smooth things over in Journalism.*

By the time Journalism rolled around, Jilly's feet were sore from her new heels. She'd worn heels only because Mr. Kortman had asked them to dress up today for their project.

Pausing at the classroom door to rest her feet, Jilly scanned the room to see who was sitting where. It looked as if Amanda had saved her a chair. That was a good sign.

Jilly hobbled toward the table. Why hadn't she thought

about wearing boots, like Amanda? They looked great with the jean dress, along with the copper-colored scarf Amanda had knotted around her neck to match the copper belt.

So Amanda had more style than she did. What else was new? Jilly tried to forget the additional fact that her friend's dress was two sizes smaller than her own.

Ignoring her sore feet, Jilly called up some last-minute enthusiasm and rushed to the table. "She did it!" Jilly exclaimed, hoping Amanda wouldn't ignore her.

"Who did what?" Amanda asked, glancing up.

"Your mom hired my parents to remodel your house."

Amanda's face broke into a smile. "I know, isn't that gr—" She stopped and stared at Jilly's dress. "Oh, no, we didn't—"

"We did."

Laughing with her best friend again felt terrific.

"Maybe no one will notice." Amanda covered the front of her dress with a large notebook, then studied Jilly. "You look really nice today."

"So do you."

"Oh, Jilly, it's neat that your parents will be working at my house. Your dad promised to work overtime so the apartment will be ready for my grandparents before Christmas."

"That's terrif—"

"What have we here?" came a familiar male voice, stopping Jilly's heart.

Jonathan Nichols grinned down at them. "You two look like the Sweet Valley twins today."

They laughed as the bell rang. Jonathan glanced about for an empty seat. No one else was at their table, so he could have sat next to either one of them. He chose the seat next to Amanda.

Jilly's heart twinged in jealousy. The truth couldn't

have been more obvious if it'd appeared as the banner headline in the *Apogee: Jonathan Nichols prefers Amanda Parks to Jilly Milford.*

Was she stupid enough to think any guy would pick her over beautiful Amanda? Why did her best friend have to be so gorgeous?

Jilly balanced her chin in her hand, grumbling to herself. *Maybe I should start hanging out with ugly girls so I'll stand out in the crowd.*

She listened while Mr. Kortman gave directions for their assignment. Today, they had to round up advertising for the school newspaper. The whole time he was talking, Amanda and Jonathan whispered and giggled together.

Jilly was close to tears by the time Mr. Kortman dismissed them. She picked up her books, planning a fast getaway before she started bawling in front of everyone.

Amanda stopped her. "Jonathan is driving me downtown. Want to come with us?"

"No." The last thing she wanted to do was ride in the back seat of Jonathan's car while he and Amanda carried on their new flirtation in the front seat.

"But Jilly, we only have the rest of the period, plus our lunch break. If you walk downtown, you won't have much time left to—"

"I said *no.*" *What's wrong with her? She knows I like Jonathan. Does she think she's doing me a favor?*

Amanda shrugged, looking puzzled. "Well, okay. See you later then."

Jilly refused to follow Amanda and Jonathan out the back door to the parking lot, so she headed toward the exit at the front of the school. There was no way she could walk all the way downtown in heels anyway, so she'd look for businesses close by.

Her heels tapped the sidewalk in a staccato rhythm as she moved at a brisk pace, needing to burn off some of the frustration she felt toward Amanda. Her friend was

39

good at turning on and off her charm. Shouldn't there be a law against flirting with a guy your best friend happens to have a mad crush on?

Jilly slipped off her heels to walk barefoot in her hose, not caring how cold the sidewalk was or what it looked like or whether or not she ran her stockings. Jealousy was such an awful feeling. She wouldn't mind if a guy was jealous over *her,* but she hated the tingling sensation inside her chest every time she pictured Jonathan and Amanda whispering together. It felt as if someone was tearing a little piece out of her heart as though it was made of red construction paper, like the ones she used to cut out for Valentine's Day.

Turning a corner, Jilly moved even faster, unaware of any businesses she might have passed. She wished she had her driver's license so she could drive and drive and drive until she calmed down. Of course, she reminded herself, she'd also need a car.

A honk and a whistle brought her back to earth. Two guys in a dilapidated Chevy slowed to grin and wave at her. Jilly grinned back—something she never did when guys were being obnoxious. But it was just the medicine she needed right now to get on with her day.

The car disappeared around a corner. Jilly squinted at the street sign in front of her. Where was she? Merrick Road and Park Boulevard. The only public buildings around here were the Bar Harbor branch of the Massapequa Library and the office of Milford Construction Company.

The library. Jilly remembered Amanda's words about researching information on people who'd lived in this community long ago. Should she give up on her Journalism assignment and do a little research on Mr. McGregor instead? It wasn't like her to skip an assignment. Well, she wouldn't skip it, she'd do it later.

Jilly turned up the next street toward the library. Wait a minute. The library would be useless to her until she found out the names of previous owners of the house on Atwater Place. What she really needed right now was a ride to the Nassau County Courthouse.

Jilly walked beyond the library to her parents' office. Pausing, she stepped into her shoes again, barged through the door, and waved to the receptionist. She found her mom in the back, watering plants.

"Jilly!" her mom exclaimed. "What are you doing here?"

"Looking for a free lunch," she answered, grinning. "And a ride to the county courthouse."

"Assignment?" Mom dumped the watering can and reached for her coat.

"More or less," Jilly answered holding the door open for her.

They ordered sandwiches-to-go from a nearby delicatessen and ate them in the car. As they neared the courthouse, Jilly tried to conceal her mounting excitement from her mother. She couldn't help wondering what she was about to discover.

Maybe that one important clue she couldn't find in her backyard this morning was hiding somewhere at the courthouse in the old records room.

41

CHAPTER 8

Jilly's mom was a familiar face at the courthouse. She stopped to visit while Jilly found the information desk and was directed to the records department.

Choosing a lady who looked as if she was in charge, Jilly explained in a hushed voice that she was interested in the names of all past owners of her house. She didn't know why she was whispering. What she was doing was perfectly legal.

The lady swiveled toward a computer screen and held out her hand to Jilly. "Let me see the tax ID number of your property."

This wasn't going to be as easy as she'd thought. "I don't have . . . I didn't bring it with me." Jilly wondered what a tax ID number was.

The lady looked at her as if she were the hundredth person who'd walked in this morning without an identification number.

"What's your name?"

"Jilly Milford."

The expression on the lady's face softened. "Ah, I just spoke to your mother up front. I'm Sally Dean, an old friend of your parents'." She smiled. "You must be inquiring about the property on Atwater."

Jilly nodded, thankful her parents were so well known in the community.

"My, your parents have been in that house for years. Are they thinking of selling?"

"No. I mean, yes." Jilly realized they'd have to put the house up for sale sooner or later if they were definitely moving to Florida.

"Oh." The lady looked sympathetic. Focusing on the computer screen, she tapped a few keys. "Let's see if we can cross-reference the property with your name and address."

In a matter of minutes, Jilly was handed a list of previous property owners. Glancing at a clock, she knew she'd have to wait until later to study the list or she wouldn't make it back to school in time for afternoon classes. Stuffing the printout sheet into her purse, she thanked the lady, then hurried off to find her mom.

After school, Jilly trudged around the last corner, heading for her house. She vowed never again to wear heels until she had a car to drive.

Voices caught her attention. Russell Talley was standing in front of her house with two strangers. Both were wearing jackets from Nassau Community College. What was going on? She quickened her steps.

"Here she comes," Russell chirped as if welcoming her to a surprise party. "Paul, Sheila, this is Jilly Milford, a resident of the house."

They beamed at her. Had she won the New York State lottery?

"Julie," Sheila began, "we're from the college TV station, and we'd like to ask you a few questions about the unusual happenings in your backyard."

Jilly's chest tightened until she could hardly breathe. "It's *Jilly.*"

Paul tapped her on the arm. "Hold on a minute. I'll get the camera." He headed toward a van parked in front of Russell's house. The logo on the side of the van said *Nassau Community College.*

A camera? Jilly glared at Russell. She was supposed to stand here and tell a TV camera all about Mr. Mc-

43

Gregor after she'd already led Russell to believe the ghost didn't exist?

Sheila pulled a clipboard from her book bag and scribbled some notes. "We'll begin by asking you some questions, then we'll move to the backyard to tape—"

"What kind of questions?" Jilly asked, forcing her voice to stay calm.

"Like, when did all this start, and—"

"When did all *what* start?"

Sheila glanced up from the clipboard. "The strange occurrences in your backyard." The girl looked at her as if she thought Jilly was incredibly dense. "Just tell us what you've seen, not what you think it is."

Jilly chose her words carefully. "I don't have any idea what you're talking about." She returned the girl's scrutiny with a smile. "Now if you'll excuse me, I have homework to do."

Sheila faced Russell as Paul returned with the camera. "What's the problem?" she asked. "I thought you said—"

"Jilly is very shy," Russell began in a condescending voice. "I think she might be worried about the camera." Sheila dropped her pencil, but before she could retrieve it, Russell grabbed it, returning it to her with a wide grin.

Smooth move, Jilly thought.

Russell was going out of his way to be polite and well mannered, adding credibility to the story he must have told them.

A blue car pulled up. Terrific. More reporters? How many had Russell called?

Paul turned the camera toward the front of her house.

"Hey," Jilly jerked on his arm. "You can't do that. I didn't give you permission to film my house."

The guy pulled away from her, steadying the camera. He glanced at Russell, then rested a brotherly hand on Jilly's shoulder. "There's no reason to be nervous." He

44

addressed her as if he were reassuring a small child. "We'll just have a brief conversation. Just relax and forget the camera is running. Don't worry about making a mistake. We can edit the tape any way we want."

Jilly heard only half of his words. The driver of the blue car was walking toward them. She couldn't take her eyes off him. He was about her age, tall, with reddish brown hair and the most penetrating aqua eyes she'd ever seen. He had a light sprinkling of freckles across his nose and cheeks. She loved guys with freckles.

All of a sudden she couldn't think of anything to say. Why hadn't she touched up her makeup before she'd left school to walk home? Probably because she *never* touched up her makeup before she left school to walk home.

"Now, Julie." Sheila's voice was brushed with irritation. "Look at me, not the camera, and simply answer the questions." She adjusted her glasses and referred to the notebook in front of her. "When did the strange sightings in your backyard first begin?"

"My name is Jilly," she said, unable to tear her eyes away from the stranger. *Who is he? What is he doing here?*

The cameraman moved in front of her, forcing her attention. Anything she said now might make it onto the college station's evening coverage of the local news—which her dad always watched.

Peering directly into the camera, Jilly took a deep breath, hoping to calm the pounding of her heart. "There seems to be some mistake." She forced a smile toward the lens. "Nothing unusual is happening here at this house. Perhaps you have the wrong address."

There, that was good. Let them show that *tonight on television. No story equals no news report.*

Jilly pivoted, heading up the walk. The cameraman followed. "Miss Milford, can you comment on your

45

neighbor's allegations of strange phenomena occurring in your backyard?''

Jilly had the perfect answer to Paul's question. All she had to say was ''Just look at my neighbor.'' But when she turned, she noticed for the first time that Russell was dressed in regular clothes. His hair was neatly combed and he was even wearing a sports jacket.

Why couldn't he have shown up in his helmet, waving his space fighter's sword and ray gun? Then they'd clearly see he was a mental case and would believe her over him.

Her clever answer caught in her throat. Now she didn't have anything to say at all. Flustered, she shifted her books into one arm and struggled to unlock the door; all the while the camera was running. Backing into the house, she shouted, ''Go away! Get off our property!''

Jilly slammed the door in the camera's lens. She dumped her books and herself into the nearest chair. ''I blew it,'' she groaned. ''Why didn't I keep up my friendly *you must have made a mistake* act? Jumping through the door and yelling *go away* certainly tips them off that something strange *is* going on.''

She wasn't sure how long she sat there. A million fears clouded her mind. If she wasn't careful, her well-kept secret would be exposed. She was in danger of losing control of the situation.

All because of Russell Talley.

The doorbell rang.

Russell!

Jilly kicked her heels across the room and jumped to her stocking feet. Russell Talley was about to get a royal piece of her mind.

Her threats started before she could get the door open. ''You jerk! What are you trying to prove? You nosy, irrespon—''

Jilly swallowed her words. Russell Talley was not

standing on her porch. The stranger from the blue car was.

He flinched, as if he feared she was going to start throwing punches.

"Um, Jilly Milford?" He took a step backward.

"Oh, it's you," she said, embarrassed by her outburst. "I—I thought you were somebody else." At least *he* got her name right.

"I hope so. I don't think you can call me a jerk since you don't even know me yet." He lowered his head as if his feelings were hurt, then raised his eyes, shooting her a mischievous wink. "That might come later."

Jilly laughed, looking beyond him to make sure both the van and Russell were gone. And to avoid the stranger's unsettling eyes.

"May I come in?"

"Yes," she stepped back, then changed her mind. "Um, I mean, no." First of all, she wasn't allowed to let anyone into the house when she was there alone after school, and secondly he was probably a reporter, although he looked too young.

"Are you a reporter?" She narrowed her eyes. *This is strictly business, Jilly. Don't get too friendly.*

He looked as if he were afraid to tell her. "I'm selling Girl Scout cookies."

"No, you're not." She swallowed a laugh.

"Okay, so I'm a reporter. Shoot me." He held his jacket open and closed his eyes in anticipation.

"Bang," Jilly said, trying to keep a serious look on her face.

"Well, now that we got that out of the way, I guess you're not up for an interview today."

"You're too young to be a reporter."

"Not for Massapequa High."

"Oh." He went to Apollo's rival high school. That meant he wasn't too old for her. *Come on, Jilly. He's here because of Mr. McGregor, not because of you.*

47

She liked interviewing him instead of vice versa. "How did you find out about these *alleged occurrences* in my backyard?" she asked, sprinkling sarcasm over her words so he'd think the allegations weren't true.

"Russ told me. We used to be neighbors."

Ah, good ol' Russell Talley, the mouth. "Why would Massapequa High want to cover this story?"

The guy looked at her as if it was obvious. "Everybody loves a good ghost story." He paused, watching her. "So, will you talk to me?" He reached one finger to trace the brass *M* on the front door.

All her feelings of panic over Russell's threat returned in a rush. "No."

He shrugged. "I understand." Pulling a piece of paper from his pocket, he scribbled on it, then gave her a sideways glance. "Well, I don't *really* understand, but I respect your right not to be interviewed. Just don't be surprised if this ends up on television tonight whether you want it to or not."

He thrust the scrap of paper at her. "Call me if you want to talk about it."

Was he giving her his phone number? Their fingers touched as she took the note. His touch warmed her so much she was surprised the paper didn't burst into flames.

"Bye." He backed down the sidewalk. "Thanks for not shooting me."

Jilly closed the door and hurried to the front window to watch him drive away. She opened the piece of paper and stared at his phone number.

Could she trust him?

No! He was a reporter. He was out to expose Mr. McGregor, just like Russell was. Crumpling the paper, she jammed it into her pocket.

Jilly slumped on the couch, taking deep breaths until her heartbeat returned to normal. She tried to stifle the

48

scenes popping into her mind, one after the other—
scenes of her and the stranger together in his blue car.

It seemed as though she'd waited all her life to open
the front door and find a guy like him waiting for her
on the porch.

But what difference did it make if someone straight
out of her dreams came knocking on her door to hand
her his phone number when it was all for the wrong
reason?

CHAPTER 9

"Jilly!"

Jilly moved to the door of the kitchen where she'd been fixing herself an evening snack. "Yes, Dad?" she hollered in answer.

"Get up here! Right now!"

She paused a moment before running up the stairs. Why all the urgency?

Taking the steps two at a time, she rounded a corner into the TV room. Her dad was standing in front of the screen, pointing at it.

Jilly arrived just in time to hear herself yelling "Get off our property!" As their front door slammed into the camera's lens, she could see the brass *M*.

Dislike for Russell bristled her insides. Why was he complicating her life like this?

Dad clicked off the set and turned to her with a stunned look on his face. "What's this all about?"

She tried to hide her anger from her father. "It's nothing, Dad."

"Nothing doesn't make it onto the evening news, Jil."

Sighing, she sat on the edge of the nearest chair. "All I know is that Russell called the TV station and told them a bunch of—" She'd started to say *lies,* but what Russell had told them was the truth. Only it was *her* truth and she didn't want anyone else to know it. "Russell told them to come out and film our backyard."

"Who's Russell?"

50

"The jerk—I mean—" She stopped, realizing her hands were balled into angry fists. "Russell is the new guy next door."

Dad sat next to her. "What *strange occurrences* were the news team referring to?"

Jilly fidgeted, wrapping the tail of her shirt around one finger. "Russell told them he'd seen some unexplained things in our backyard."

"Like what?"

"Like strange lights. And movements." She hadn't actually heard Russell say those things, but she assumed that's what he'd been seeing.

"Doesn't this young man think we'd know if something odd was happening in our own backyard?"

Jilly shrugged, hating Russell for putting her into this position.

Dad rose. "I'll call and have a chat with his parents."

She started to protest, then decided it might slow Russell down if his parents disapproved. "Can I go back to my homework now?" *Groan. Asking Dad if she could go back to her homework was a dead giveaway that something major was wrong.*

"Sure."

Jilly made a beeline for the door as her mom entered the room.

"Wait." Dad paused, as if trying to tie up loose ends. "Does all this have anything to do with those stories you used to tell when Grandpa Milford was alive? About the ghost? Have you been talking about it again?" He looked disappointed, as if he'd believed his little girl had grown up, only to discover she was still a seven-year-old.

"No, Dad. I haven't talked about that in years." To anyone except Amanda, she added to herself. "I don't talk to Russell at all." She wrinkled her nose and stuck out her tongue so her dad would know exactly what she thought of their new neighbor.

51

"Would someone please tell me what's going on?" Mom asked, eyes flitting back and forth between the two of them.

Dad waved Jilly away. She was grateful he wasn't going to make her sit through another explanation.

The next day Amanda met Jilly at her locker to walk her to Journalism. Jilly vowed to be cool about her friend hanging out with Jonathan Nichols. She couldn't handle more than one day a week of Amanda not speaking to her.

Excitement over Jilly's parents working at Amanda's house kept them making big plans for the weekend. It would almost be like they were living together, real sisters in a big family.

As they made their way down the hall, Amanda's jabbering stopped in mid-word. Jilly glanced up to see the reason why. Kevin Dobbins was approaching. Next to him was Traci Wooster. A sidelong glance confirmed the hurt look she knew would be on Amanda's face.

When they got close enough, Jilly called out, "Hey, Kevin. Hello!"

Kevin acted as if he'd just seen them for the first time that instant. "Oh, hello, Amanda," he called back. Traci gave them a blank stare.

Jilly tried to ignore the fact that she'd been the one to say hello, but it was Amanda whom Kevin had answered.

She was afraid to look at her friend. Had she made her mad again? Nope, she was grinning. Good sign, Jilly thought.

"Did you hear that?" Amanda whispered. "He said hello to me. In front of Traci." She laughed. "That's the first time all week." She squeezed Jilly's arm. "Thanks for doing that, friend."

Amanda was on cloud nine during Journalism. Their

table was full, so Jonathan couldn't join them. Jilly was relieved. Amanda didn't even notice.

Everyone scribbled away on their assignment to write ad copy for the businesses they'd sold newspaper space to yesterday. Amanda was busy on her ad for Carvel Ice Cream, which is where she and Jonathan had ended up.

Jilly glanced around the room, hoping Mr. Kortman didn't notice she was the only one not writing. She was usually the first to finish in-class assignments, but yesterday she'd spent her time working on a project that seemed to be consuming her life.

Maybe she could write an ad for the courthouse, since that's where she'd gone. She laughed to herself. What would the ad be for? Bail bonds to get out of jail? *Brilliant Jilly. How many kids at Apollo High needed bail bonds?*

What other businesses had she seen yesterday? Her parents'. Ah! Her parents! The Milford Construction Company! Why hadn't she thought of it before? She wouldn't even need to ask her dad for the ad money. She could pay it out of her own allowance. Her parents wouldn't have to know the advertisement ran at all.

Jilly pulled out a fresh piece of paper and a ruler to draw a border around the ad. Then she wrote:

The Milford Construction Company
Serving Massapequa since 1974
We specialize in:

custom building   innovative designs

remodeling   fire damage

sky lights   winterproofing

decks and patios   roof repair

Pleased, Jilly designed an eye catching logo: $\overset{M_C}{C}$ then turned in her assignment. She really didn't know what her parents' company specialized in, but she knew they'd done all the things listed.

Suddenly, Jilly had the urge to make up another ad. One that read, "Hire Russell Talley, ghost exterminator. He'll pulverize your poltergeists with one laser beam from his ray gun. Work guaranteed."

That should discredit him in front of the entire student body, Jilly thought, chuckling to herself. And a copy of the ad, mailed anonymously to the college TV station, should take care of the rest of the community.

Jilly's temptation passed quickly. She really wasn't the vengeful type. Let Russell Talley discredit himself by his own weirdness. She had better things to do.

Like dream about the stranger in the blue car.

CHAPTER 10

Jilly couldn't get home fast enough after school. She planned to spend the night at Amanda's since her parents were working there. But she'd left her overnight bag home—on purpose—so she'd have a reason to go there alone. She wanted time to explore her backyard during daylight hours after being scared out of her skin yesterday in the early morning darkness.

Slipping into jeans and a comfortable sweater, Jilly set her overnight bag by the front door, pulled on a heavy jacket and gloves, then headed out to the backyard.

Again she walked, tracing Mr. McGregor's steps from the toolshed to the gazebo, the gazebo to the canal, the canal back to the toolshed—all the while keeping her ears peeled for the sound of Russell Talley's moped arriving home.

The eerie feeling which had smothered her last time she explored the yard did not return, perhaps staved off by the light of day. This was the yard in which she'd spent countless hours all the summers of her life, and she knew it as well as she knew her own bedroom.

Jilly had already explored the gazebo, there was nothing to see in the canal, so that left the toolshed. Her dad kept extra keys on a ring, hanging over a nail in the basement stairwell. Returning to the house, Jilly opened the basement door and grabbed the key ring. Something on the wall next to the nail caught her eye. The double heart sign was carved into the wood.

Jilly froze. Had it always been there? Why hadn't she noticed it before?

She traced the tiny hearts with her fingers. The wall was unpainted plasterboard, so there was no telling how long the hearts had been there.

When she was younger, Dad would send her to fetch the keys to the toolshed for him so he could get out the rakes. It'd been years since she'd helped her dad with yard work. She remembered having to stand on her tiptoes to reach the key ring. Maybe the hearts had always been there, but she'd never been tall enough to see them before.

Or maybe it was a sign.

A sign? *Come on, Jilly. You've been watching too many old reruns of* "The Twilight Zone."

Grabbing the keys, she returned to the backyard and unlocked the toolshed. The thin wooden door creaked open, late afternoon sun spilling across the floor. Musty air mingled with fresh air as the breeze swept inside.

The shed housed a small workbench. Her dad had used it when he first started his construction business. Then he'd built a larger, more modern workroom in their basement and moved all his tools and supplies downstairs. Now Dad had a regular office near the school so the shed served as a junk room and a place to store snow shovels, rakes, gardening equipment, and a few boxes of old Christmas ornaments.

For a while Jilly had used the shed as a clubhouse. She'd lettered a sign to read "For girls only. No boys allowed." Glancing around, she wondered what had happened to the sign after all these years.

When her girls' club had gotten too large, they'd moved their meetings to the gazebo, but then the boys in the neighborhood showed up to taunt them. The meetings would be forgotten while the girls chased the boys away.

Then the club decided it was more fun having the boys around than chasing them away. About the same time, the boys decided it was more fun to ride bikes and skateboards than to hang out with girls.

Holding meetings with no chance of a boy attack turned out not to be as much fun, so the club dwindled away until she and Amanda were the only members left.

Jilly examined every inch of the ancient shed, all the while trying not to get to dirty. Everything was coated with years of dust and dirt.

Nothing seemed unusual or out of place. Kneeling, she explored the floor under the workbench.

Nothing.

A shaft of light made the dust particles close to the floor shimmer and dance. Jilly traced her finger through the thin layer of sand which had sifted through cracks in the walls year after year. *J.A.M.* She drew a heart around her initials. It reminded her of the tiny double hearts, so she traced another heart in the sand, barely touching hers. Instinctively she reached to print *J.N.* inside the heart for Jonathan Nichols, then paused as the stranger in the blue car came to mind.

Why did she keep thinking about him? Laughing at herself, she traced the initials S.I.T.B.C. in tiny letters inside the second heart: *Stranger In The Blue Car.*

As she stood, her eye caught the faint shadow of a raised board in the floor. She'd never noticed it before. It must have gotten warped from all the rain they'd had this fall.

Dropping to her knees again, Jilly brushed sand away. The board was not nailed down. She lifted it with one finger, discovering a hollowed-out place underneath.

Excited, Jilly jumped to her feet to move the lawnmower outside so it was not in the way. Then she grabbed a broom and swept the floor clean.

The sun had shifted, making it darker in the shed. She pulled the long string hanging from the bare bulb above her, clicking on the light. Jilly removed the board easily, peering into the dark hole.

Inside was a metal box that looked as if it hadn't seen the light of day for decades. Spiderwebs tied it to the earthen walls of the hole. The box appeared to be nestled in angel hair, like her mom put on their Christmas tree.

Ignoring the squeamish feeling spiderwebs gave her, Jilly grabbed the broom again and cleaned them away. Gingerly, she reached into the hole, jiggling the box sideways until it came through the narrow opening. Setting it on the floor, she brushed away the rest of the spiderwebs.

The rusted lock fell apart in Jilly's hand. She pulled off the bolt, letting the pieces crumble to the floor.

Holding her breath, she opened the lid, not sure what she was about to find. Money? Jewels? A treasure map?

Papers. The box was full of papers, stiff from years of moisture and heat alternating with freezing temperatures.

Jilly unfolded the first sheet. It was a letter:

My dearest Molly,
Altho your eyes will never read these words, I must pen my love for you or my heart will surely burst. Day after day, I watch over you like a guardian angel, trying to hide what I feel inside. Earth has never known a creature more lovely than you. I live for the day I might tell you how I feel.

Yours,
Caleb

Molly? Caleb? Who are they? Or who *were* they? Jilly wondered, thinking back to the list of previous owners she'd gotten from the courthouse. Even though she'd given it only a quick glance, all the names listed were men's, yet she didn't recall the name *Caleb*.

Suddenly aware of the passage of time, Jilly quickly scanned a few more letters. Amanda would be wondering why she hadn't shown up at her house yet, and her parents would start to worry, too.

The notes, letters, and a few poems, seemed to be out of order. A Christmas card, never sent, followed a Valentine poem. Then a letter mentioned the soft nights of summer. One Jilly didn't understand at all. It simply said:

Molly, oh Molly, why? How could I not . . .

The ink was smeared as if rain had fallen onto the page. Or tears. *How could I not what?* Jilly opened the next note.

"Mowing your lawn in December?" came a voice from behind, startling her.

Jilly froze when she recognized the voice as Russell's. Trying to act casual, she returned the unfinished letter to the metal box and closed the lid. Rising, she blocked Russell's view of the missing board, in spite of his leaning one way and then the other to get a look behind her.

"What do you want?" she demanded, forcing him backward, away from the inside of the shed.

"You seem to have an unusual interest in something in there." He pointed, attempting to step around her, but she moved to block his way.

"So what?" she snapped. "This is *my* shed in *my* backyard and you're trespassing on *my* property."

Russell backed off, kicking at the wheel of the lawnmower. He was dressed normally again today. But then, he'd just gotten home from school. Maybe he hadn't had time to change into his weird space creature clothes.

"Why are you so unfriendly to me?" he asked, looking miffed, acting almost like a regular person for a change.

"Because you're invading my privacy. You called a TV station. How can you expect me to be your friend after you did that?"

"Why won't you work together with me on this?"

"On what?"

Russell's face turned from a smile to a scowl. The wrinkles emphasized his scar. "Stop playing ignorant, Jilly. It's obvious you're hiding something."

"No I'm not."

"Then let me have a look inside the tool shed." He stepped toward her. She grabbed the doorway with one hand, barring his entry.

"If you're not hiding anything, why won't you let me in?"

Jilly knew she'd discovered something important hidden under the loose board. If she let Russell see the letters, it would add more fuel to the fire he'd already started. She needed time to figure out what the letters meant, and who Molly and Caleb were.

Stepping back into the shed to stall him, her eyes fell on something familiar wedged between the workbench and the wall. She yanked at it until it came free, then held it up proudly to Russell.

It was a sign, written in the squiggly hand of a third grader: *For girls only. No boys aloud.* She'd forgotten about the misspelled word.

Cocking her head at Russell, she smiled. "Got to do what the sign says."

He pointed a bony finger at her. "I will find out what's going on around here. It's my mission."

"Mission?" she repeated, wrinkling her nose.

"With you or without you, the truth shall be known." He gave his standard salute, touching two fingers to his scar. "Full tanks and no turbulence." Turning, he ran toward the gate separating their backyards.

Jilly waited until he was out of sight. She tossed the sign onto the bench and grabbed a handful of letters from the box, stuffing them into her jacket pocket. Closing the lid, she returned the box to the hole and replaced the warped board.

Quickly she rolled the lawnmower back into place, adjusting it to hide her discovery. Making sure the toolshed was locked tight, she dashed into the house, hung up the key ring, grabbed her overnight bag, then tore out the front door for Amanda's house.

A glance toward Russell's yard stopped her heart, even though her feet kept running. Parked in front of the Talley's house was the blue car. Next to that was a station wagon with a logo on the side for *Newsday,* Long Island's daily newspaper.

Jilly's anger smoldered inside, despite the sight of the blue car. This was turning into a battle—not between her and Russell Talley, but between her and the world.

As she ran toward Amanda's house, her footsteps beat the same rhythm over and over against the sidewalk: *Mr. McGregor will stay forever. Mr. McGregor will stay forever.*

Jilly hoped it was true.

CHAPTER 11

Jilly ran all the way to Amanda's house.

The sound of hammering and sawing led her to the backyard. Dad was on a ladder helping a carpenter frame the new addition. Normally he didn't do the work himself, but, because of the slump in business, he'd laid off most of the workers, and was doing a lot of the small jobs on his own. Jilly caught his eye and waved.

"There you are!" Amanda almost plowed into her. She was carrying her little sister Hollianne out to watch the workers.

"Where've you been?" she asked, setting Hollianne on the ground and giving her strict orders to stay far away from the bustling activity.

"I had to go home and pack my overnight bag." It wasn't a total lie, Jilly told herself. Should she tell Amanda about the letters? And about the TV crew showing up at her house? There was no reason not to. The plan to research Mr. McGregor had been Amanda's idea in the first place. Maybe she'd have some good advice.

"Can we go to your room?" Jilly asked, glad for someone to confide in.

"Well, it's about time you told me about it."

"About what?" *How could Amanda know? She must have watched the local news last night.*

"We need to talk." Amanda grabbed Hollianne's hand. "Let's go inside."

Jilly followed the two inside, stopping to say hello to

her mom and Mrs. Parks. Both were hunched over Mom's blueprints of the new apartment and barely looked up to acknowledge the girls.

Amanda urged Jilly down the hallway to her room, shutting the door to keep her little sister out. She clicked on her stereo, adjusting the volume so they could talk, then sat on the floor.

Jilly joined her. They always sat on the floor in Amanda's room because the thick carpet, a soft powder blue, was much more comfortable than a chair.

"So, why didn't you tell me?" Amanda began.

"I don't understand how you found out."

"Your dad told me."

"He did?" Jilly was surprised. She thought her dad would want to forget the whole thing. "My dad told you I was on the news last night?"

Amanda stared at her. "You were on the news?"

"Isn't that what you're talking about?"

"No. Your dad told us you're moving to Florida."

"Oh, that."

Amanda rolled onto her side, crooking her elbow to rest her head. "We're best friends, yet you don't even tell me you're moving away. What were you going to do? Leave a note in my locker? So long. Good-bye. It's been nice knowing you?"

Before Jilly could respond, Amanda rushed on, "But what's all this about being on the news last night?"

Jilly sighed. "One problem at a time, please. I haven't been able to talk to anyone about moving to Florida. Sometimes I think not talking about it will make it not happen."

"It would be terrible if you moved. What would I do?" Amanda grabbed a stuffed white walrus from a nearby pile of raggedy cloth animals and hugged it to her chest.

"Be best friends with Traci Wooster?"

"No thank you." She threw the walrus at Jilly. "Get on with the rest of your story."

"My life is being terrorized by my new neighbor," Jilly began, then told Amanda about Russell Talley, the TV news story, and the stranger in the blue car.

"I want to meet this Russell Talley. I can't believe I haven't seen him around school. He sounds too weird."

"He is."

"And I definitely want to meet the stranger in the blue car."

Jilly's insides knotted at Amanda's words and the expression on her face. Guys always picked Amanda over her.

But I saw him first, she told herself, and he really affected me—especially my heart rate and my blood pressure.

If the stranger in the blue car meets Amanda, he'll never give me another look. Of course he hasn't given me a look to begin with, but he's so nice . . .

"Hello?" Amanda waved a plaid stuffed mouse in front of her face.

Jilly tried to hide her thoughts. Her friend couldn't help it if guys were drawn to her as if she wore gravity for perfume.

She was unsure whether or not to tell the rest of the story—about the loose board and the letters. Jilly knew she couldn't wait much longer to read the ones she'd stashed in her jacket pocket, so she decided to tell.

Amanda sat like a statue, listening to the story. When Jilly finished, Amanda hopped to her feet to snatch Jilly's jacket off her bed, yanking the letters from the pocket. "Let's read them right now."

"Wait." Jilly rescued the letters from Amanda's grasp. "I think we need to be a little more solemn about this. After all, we're trespassing in someone else's life."

Amanda pretended to act solemn, tiptoeing back to

64

her spot on the carpet and arranging a serious look on her face.

Jilly laughed at her. That was one big difference between them. Jilly had to do everything slowly and ponderously while Amanda jumped in the middle and took it from there. She stacked the letters in a pile, one by one, smoothing out the crinkles.

"So what do the letters have to do with Mr. McGregor?" Amanda asked.

"I'm not sure. Maybe nothing." Jilly opened her purse to recover the list of names identifying the previous owners of her house. She scanned the page. "There's no one here named Caleb." A feeling of disappointment tugged at her. She'd hoped Caleb's full name would be on the list to assuage her curiosity, but it wasn't.

Jilly rolled onto her stomach to study the names and dates. Amanda read over her shoulder. The Atwater house had been built in 1931 by the original owner, Samuel Harrigan. After 1956, there'd been a string of owners, some staying longer than others. Then, after 1962, the house stood empty until the Milfords bought it in 1974.

Jilly remembered her parents' tales of the terrible shape the house had been in when they bought it. No wonder it'd remained empty for twelve years, Jilly thought. Her dad and mom, newly married, remodeled the entire house—Milford Construction Company's first job. By the time Jilly was born, the house was almost completely redone.

"This list is useless to me," Jilly said, sighing. "Who was Caleb if not one of the owners? And why did he have access to the toolshed? He must have spent a lot of time there or he never would've hollowed out the space under the floor to hide his personal letters." She tossed the list aside. "And who was Molly?"

Amanda took hold of the back of Jilly's neck, signifying that her patience had evaporated. "If you don't

65

show me the letters right now," she said through clenched teeth, "I'm going to die and become a ghost and haunt your bedroom for the rest of your life."

"Okay, okay." Jilly set the pile of letters between them. She felt bad that she'd crumpled some of them in her haste as they were already in fragile condition.

Amanda grabbed one.

"Wait," Jilly caught her hand. "Let's read them together."

"You're so *slow*. Come on. This is the mystery of the year."

Jilly flattened the first page. It was a poem, addressed to *Molly, my heart's secret:*

"Come away, come, sweet love!
The golden morning breaks;
All the earth, all the air of love and pleasure speaks.
Teach thine arms then to embrace,
And sweet rosy lips to kiss,
And mix our souls in mutual bliss;
Eyes were made for beauty's grace,
Viewing, ruing love-long pain,
Procured by beauty's rude disdain."

Amanda flopped onto her back. "Gad, how romantic. *'Mix our souls in mutual bliss.'* Did Caleb write that? He's good."

Jilly was relating to the *'love-long pain'* line. She scanned the rest of the page. "No, he says it was written a long time ago by an anonymous poet from the 16th century. Listen to this note he added at the end: *I, a humble man, cannot express my love for you. Only the words of a great poet can. Will I show these lines to you? Time will tell. For now you'll remain . . . my deepest heart's secret."*

Jilly read the words a few more times, then refolded the poem tenderly. Each time she came to the words

66

heart's secret, chill bumps attacked her body. "Boy, Mr. McGregor was really in love with this Molly person."

Amanda came to her knees. "Did you hear what you just said? You said *Mr. McGregor* was in love with Molly. Jil, it's *Caleb* who's in love with Molly, not Mr. McGregor." Her eyes flashed. "Or are you thinking the same thing I'm thinking?"

"That Mr. McGregor is—or was—Caleb?"

They both dived for the letters at the same time, looking for more clues. Jilly copied dates, each time one was mentioned. Most of them ranged from 1932 to 1941.

"Wow," Jilly whispered. "Almost ten years of longing for someone in secret must have been—"

"Look!" Amanda thrust another letter into Jilly's face. "This one says, 'Samuel is the luckiest man in the world'."

"Samuel?" Jilly hadn't thought about anyone else being part of the story. "You mean after all Caleb's agony, Molly married someone named Samuel?"

Amanda grabbed the list of previous homeowners. "It's here. Look! A man named Samuel Harrigan was the builder and original owner of your house."

"That means Samuel was in the picture long before Caleb started writing letters to Molly. Except . . ."

"Except what?"

"We don't have all the letters. I took only a handful."

"Maybe we have all we need."

"What do you mean?"

Amanda glanced at her watch. "Come on, we still have time to call the courthouse before they close for the weekend."

"But we already know Samuel owned the house."

"Yes, but we don't know what his wife's name was."

"Ah, ha," Jilly said, catching on. "His marriage license would be on file."

Jilly and Amanda raced each other down the hall to the phone. As Amanda looked up the number, Jilly wondered about the heaviness settling inside her chest. Poor Caleb. Had he been in love with another man's wife? Had he died of lovesickness, then returned to haunt the home of his beloved?

A sudden chill passed through Jilly. Or was he returning to her yard night after night, year after year, trying to retrieve the letters he wrote six decades ago to Molly? Was he unhappy that Jilly had found them?

Maybe he *wanted* her to find them, she argued with herself. Was it merely a coincidence that she discovered the loose board after all these years? Or had Mr. McGregor somehow led her to find it?

Jilly leaned her head against the wall as Amanda punched in the phone number to the courthouse. "Mr. McGregor," she whispered under her breath, "did you write these letters and hide them in the toolshed? Is your real name Caleb?"

Jilly had a feeling she was about to find out.

CHAPTER 12

"Bull's-eye." Amanda set the phone on its hook and faced Jilly. "Samuel Harrigan married Molly Dilger on August 25, 1931."

"Call them back."

"What?" Amanda looked confused. "It has to be right, Jil. The lady—"

"Call them back." Jilly glanced at her watch. The courthouse closed for the weekend in three minutes. "While you were talking, I looked at the list again. We missed something important."

"What?" Amanda started to look.

"Dial!"

"I forgot the number."

"Look it up."

Amanda fumbled with the phone book, "What am I supposed to say when they answer?"

"Ask for . . ." Jilly closed her eyes. What was the name of the lady who'd helped her look up previous homeowners?

"Hurry, it's ringing."

"Sally something."

"May I please speak to Sally something?"

Jilly jabbed her in the side. "This is serious."

Amanda covered her mouth to keep from laughing into the phone. She listened for a moment. "I know the courthouse is closing, ma'am, but this is very, very important." She paused. "No, it can't wait until Monday. Why am I calling? Um . . ."

Jilly grabbed the phone, explaining who she was to Sally. "The first homeowner's name is listed in 1931," she explained. "Then, in the fine print after his name, there's a description of the lot, the square footage of the house, and all that. But at the very end, it says ownership of the property was transferred into Molly Harrigan's name on December 31, 1931, Code 14. What does that mean?"

"Simple. Code 14 means that the second party inherited the property."

"Thank you very much." Jilly put the phone back on the hook.

"Tell me. Tell me." Amanda jumped up and down three times.

"Girls! Time to eat!" came Mrs. Parks's voice.

Jilly folded the list and put it into her pocket. "Molly inherited the house from Samuel."

"Inherited? You mean . . . ?"

"Yep. Samuel must have died. Right after they were married."

"Wow."

They stared at each other as the news sunk in.

"So," Amanda whispered as Hollianne toddled down the hall toward them, "the love letters Caleb wrote to Molly were written *after* Samuel was out of the picture."

"Right. He fell in love with a widow."

"Girls!"

"Coming!" Amanda hollered back. She turned her sister in the direction of the dining room and nudged her forward. "There's something I still don't understand."

"What?"

"We've figured out who Molly and Samuel were. But we still don't know who Caleb is—was."

70

Jilly agreed. He was the one she was most curious about. "How can we find out?"

"The library. Tomorrow. We've got the date of their marriage, but we'll have to look through a lot of old papers to find a death notice."

"No we won't. Samuel must have died in the fall or early winter, since they were married in August and the property ownership was transferred at the end of the year."

"Good deduction, Sherlock," Amanda said, patting her on the back.

"Thank you, Watson. Solving mysteries makes me hungry. Let's eat."

Amanda and Jilly arrived at the Massapequa Library as soon as it opened the next morning. They settled themselves into a corner of the reference room in front of a microfilm viewer.

The technology of reducing newspapers to microfilm obviously wasn't around in 1931. The papers were preserved on film, but they'd deteriorated so much before the procedure became common, the words were hard to read.

Still, Jilly easily found the wedding announcement and even a picture of Molly as a seventeen-year-old bride. The picture was hard to make out clearly, but the faded photograph of the unsmiling, makeup-free Molly Dilger, dressed in white lace, jolted Jilly. "Gosh," she whispered to Amanda. "It's hard to believe she was a real person who lived right here in Massapequa."

It also surprised her that Molly had been only two years older than she and Amanda when she married. "People certainly got married a lot younger back then."

Amanda studied the picture. "They didn't smile for the camera in those days, either."

"She was pretty." Jilly whispered, feeling a need to

71

defend Molly for some reason. "No wonder both Samuel and Caleb were in love with her."

Amanda cocked her head. "I think a little mascara and blusher might help her looks a lot. And maybe a perm."

Jilly laughed, shooting a glance at one of the library workers in apology.

A long article accompanied Molly's picture. It began the same as any other wedding announcement, Jilly noticed, her eyes skimming the blurred words.

"Look!"

Jilly read ahead to see what Amanda was pointing at.

Amanda read aloud, *"Mr. Harrigan's best man, Caleb Hart, helped Samuel Harrigan build a new home for his bride and will be employed by the Harrigans as the groundskeeper."*

Jilly's eyes met Amanda's. "So, Caleb was a friend of the family. And Samuel hired him as a groundskeeper."

"What's a groundskeeper? A gardener? Your yard isn't big enough to warrant a gardener."

"Oh, the house used to be on three acres. My dad told me. There were no houses on either side for a long time. The property even continued on the other side of the canal. Dad said there used to be a bridge, but when more people built in the area, the bridge was removed so people could sail boats down the canal."

Amanda continued to study the microfilm. "Let's see if we can find out how Samuel died."

Meticulously, they scanned the papers from the last few months of 1931 until they found it. The picture showed a handsome man in a stand-up collar and bow tie. The article said in part: *"Taken before his time, Samuel Anthony Harrigan, 25, was killed by a fall from his horse during a fox hunt. He is survived by his wife, Molly. There are no children."*

Jilly's heart ached at the thought of such a tragedy

happening to someone so young. But then, Molly still had Caleb. Had she married him? Or had Caleb ever gotten up enough nerve to tell Molly he loved her? Maybe Molly never knew she was Caleb's *heart's secret*.

"Good morning."

The voice jolted Jilly out of the past and into the present. She glanced up. Kevin Dobbins smiled down at them.

Jilly could feel Amanda tense beside her.

"What are you doing here?" Amanda said, recovering fast enough to slip into her flirtatious mode.

Kevin shuffled a handful of books. "I got a job here, working Saturday mornings and a few days after school."

He and Amanda grinned at each other until Jilly wanted to disappear. She reread Samuel Harrigan's obituary notice three times.

After a few minutes of listening to their small talk, Jilly got the distinct feeling she was preventing them from talking about *more serious things*. Maybe Kevin wanted to invite Amanda back to the alley behind 7-Eleven so he could kiss her again on the brick wall beside the dumpsters.

Only Kevin couldn't ask Amanda as long as Jilly was in the way.

She collected the microfilm and gathered her things.

"Are you leaving?" Amanda asked, feigning surprise. They'd planned on spending most of the day together, since Jilly's parents were working at Amanda's house again. Mrs. Parks had promised to drive them to the mall later. But Jilly decided to be a good friend and make herself scarce so Amanda's afternoon would be free for Kevin Dobbins.

"I gotta lot to do today," she lied. "And I already found the information I needed here." Jilly gave them both a quick wave. "See you later."

As she walked home, Jilly mulled over the story of

Samuel, Molly, and Caleb. It was almost like reading a novel about the three, but the story was being given to her one page at a time. She was eager to read ahead and find out what happened, but she had to search for every page.

Caleb was such a romantic. *Am I ever going to find a guy who loves me as much as Caleb loved Molly?*

The image of the stranger in the blue car drove across her mind. If Molly was Caleb's *heart's secret,* then the stranger was hers. *Heart's secret.* She liked the sound of the words.

Suddenly she remembered the tiny double hearts engraved in hidden corners around the house and yard. Caleb's last name was Hart. Was Caleb the one who'd etched them? Maybe somewhere in the remaining notes and letters she'd find the answer.

Jilly was almost beside herself with curiosity as she hurried home. Since her parents were at Amanda's, she could open the shed without anyone asking questions. There had to be another clue, still to be uncovered, that would link Caleb Hart to Mr. McGregor.

In her excitement to read more of the letters, Jilly began to run, arriving home out of breath—and starving. She and Amanda had planned to eat lunch at the mall, but now that was off. Should she make herself a sandwich or go get the rest of the letters first?

Go get the rest of the letters first, a voice inside her head answered. Swinging through the kitchen, Jilly's eyes fell upon a note, scrawled in her dad's handwriting:

Jilly,
In case you beat us home, I wanted you to know I called the parents of that boy next door. They were concerned and said they'd talk to him. He was very polite to me, even offered to rake the yard.

Later,
Your Father

Jilly chuckled at the signature. Dad always signed letters and cards to her "Your Father."

So, Russell had made a good impression on Dad. Even offered to rake the yard. Jilly dropped the note. Rake the yard? Russell wasn't being neighborly. He wanted access to the toolshed!

She raced to the basement stairs and flung open the door. The keys dangled from their hook. Quickly she searched for the one that unlocked the toolshed, feeling relieved to find it there.

But Russell must have taken the key or he wouldn't have been able to get the rakes out of the shed. What if he . . . ?

Frantic, Jilly rushed out the door to the shed, fumbling with the lock. Why did she feel that someone was watching her? Shrugging it off, she yanked at the lock until it came free. Fresh footsteps showed on the dusty floor. Jilly yanked the lawnmower out of the way, then knelt and lifted the loose board.

Relief flooded over her when she saw the metal box. He hadn't found it! Turning it on its side, she pulled the box from the hole. Gingerly she released the latch, feeling once more that she was imposing on someone else's life, or even taking a trip backward in time.

As the lid came open, Jilly caught her breath.

The box was empty.

The rest of the letters were gone.

CHAPTER 13

Taking a deep breath, Jilly gave the Talley's front door three firm knocks to show she meant business. This was not a social call.

Be tactful, she said to herself. You can't start yelling at him the minute he opens the door or he'll get defensive and maybe even deny that he took the letters.

Jilly knocked again, swallowing the urge to cry. Every time she got mad at someone, she felt like crying. It made her angry with herself. She wished she could confront people and let them know when they'd hurt, betrayed, or insulted her, but tears would come instead, and she'd end up embarrassing herself.

As she raised her fist to knock again, the door clicked open. A thin, gray-haired lady appeared. Russell's grandmother?

"May I please speak to Russell?" Jilly heard her voice quiver as the urge to cry knotted in her throat. She attempted a smile at the woman to be polite, but was too upset to smile.

"Why, you're the young lady next door," the woman exclaimed.

Jilly nodded. *Be nice. She's not the one who's made you angry.*

The lady extended a hand. "I'm Lydia Talley, Russell's mother."

Mother? Jilly shook her hand.

"Russell isn't home right now, but he'll be *so* pleased that you stopped by to see him."

Right. He's probably hiding under his bed for fear I'll attack him with his plastic space fighter's sword.

"Thank you." Jilly took a step backward.

"Would you like Russell to call you when he gets home?"

"No," Jilly blurted. "I—I'll see him around."

"Drop by any time."

"Thank you, Mrs. Talley, I will." Jilly laughed at her own comment. Russell was the last person in the neighborhood—in the *galaxy*—she wanted to drop in on.

Returning home, Jilly stationed herself by the front window to watch for Russell. She tried to read a magazine, but all she could think about was the melancholy love story of Molly and Caleb.

Jilly's heart broke for them. Did they ever get together? It was driving her crazy. She had to find out. The answer was probably hidden right there in the rest of the letters, but now she'd never know.

Yes, she would. Those letters belonged to her. Well, they didn't actually belong to her. Maybe she could say she inherited them.

Jilly was dying to talk to Amanda, both to tell her about the disappearance of the letters and to find out what happened with Kevin Dobbins. But she was afraid to call Amanda's house, just in case she was still out with Kevin. If Mrs. Parks thought the two of them were together, then she didn't want to get her friend into trouble.

Just as Jilly stood up to move to the kitchen for something to eat, she heard a car. Kneeling on the sofa, she pulled back the curtain to look. The now-familiar blue car was stopping in front of the Talleys' house.

Jilly waited. Russell stepped out, waved, and started up the walk. He was carrying a large manila envelope.

77

The letters? She hoped he hadn't been out showing them to the TV stations and the newspapers.

Squinting, she tried to make out the driver of the blue car. Of course she knew who it was, but she just wanted another glimpse of him. Her heart twinged as he started up his car. So near, yet so far away.

The car moved forward, slowed, then stopped in front of her house.

Jilly's heart stopped along with the car. He was coming to see her!

Jumping off the couch, she raced to the hall mirror. Her hair was a mess! She never bothered with much makeup on Saturdays, and her clothes! Why had she worn her dad's old shirt over the sweats which were too baggy on her?

Dashing down the hall, she swung into the guest bathroom, grabbing a comb from the drawer. As she yanked it through her hair, the doorbell rang. Jilly tucked in the shirt. It made her waist look twice as thick as it was. She pulled the shirt out, then leaned close to the mirror to inspect her face. There was nothing wrong with it that thirty minutes with an Avon lady wouldn't fix. Except she didn't have an Avon lady hanging around the house and she didn't have thirty minutes.

The bell rang again.

Should she pretend she wasn't home? *And miss the chance of seeing him again?*

What if he never came back? *Give him a reason to come back, Jilly.*

She waited a few seconds.

Silence. Had he gone?

A knock sounded. She grimaced at herself in the mirror. "He didn't come to see *you,* Jilly Milford, he came to see the girl who happens to live in this house. He could care less what *she* looks like."

Jilly ran to the living room, then stopped to catch her breath before opening the door.

He filled the whole door frame, he was so tall. His face crinkled as his aqua eyes smiled down upon her.

"Hi. I was beginning to think your doorbell was on the blink."

"I—I was busy. Upstairs." Jilly pointed up, hoping he'd believe the house was so huge, it took her six whole minutes to get to the front door.

"May I come in this time?"

Jilly paused, then decided she'd better obey her mom's rules in order to stay home alone in the afternoons.

"My parents aren't here, and I'm not allowed to—"

He held up a hand. "It's okay. My parents are the same way."

He turned around. Was he leaving? Jilly's heart sank.

"I could go for a walk," she ventured. What was she saying? He wanted to quiz her about Mr. McGregor. She should refuse to talk to him at all.

He pivoted toward her. "I've got an idea. I haven't eaten lunch yet. Why don't we run out and grab a bite, and . . . are you hungry?"

"Starved." Jilly smiled at him. It was almost a date!

"Let's go, then."

"Could you wait a minute while I change?"

"You look great."

"I do?" *Was he blind?*

"Yeah."

"I can do better than this," she said, gesturing toward her clothes. "Three minutes?"

He nodded, stepping toward the door, then stopped, remembering. "I'll just wait out here."

She closed the door, knowing it wasn't very polite to make him wait outside on the porch, but rules were rules.

Racing upstairs, Jilly tore off her baggy outfit, grabbed her best blue jeans and a red sweater. Dad always told her that red was her color.

She combed her hair again and put on mascara as fast

as she could with a shaking hand. A dab of makeup and blush, some dangling earrings, a touch of cherry-colored lip gloss and she was ready. Wait. She squirted some of her mom's perfume in her hair, then raced into the bathroom for a swig of mouthwash—just in case.

Jilly tried to hurry down the stairs without bouncing and messing up her hair. Should she leave her parents a note? What if they found out she wasn't with Amanda and she wasn't at home? They'd be worried.

Grabbing the note pad and pencil from beside the phone, she realized more than three minutes had passed. What if the stranger in the blue car had gotten tired of waiting and left without her?

Jilly rushed through the living room and peeked out the peep hole in the front door. He was still there, looking bored.

She opened the door. "Sorry I took so long. I still need to jot a note for my parents. She started to write, then stopped, feeling his eyes on her, looking her up and down. Did she meet with his approval?

"Dear Mom and Dad," he began, dictating the note to her.

She laughed. He'd noticed she was having a hard time deciding what to write.

"Since you don't allow me to let strangers into the house," he continued. *"I didn't think you'd mind if a stranger lured me into his strange car with the promise of a strange meal and some strange conversation."*

Jilly laughed again, resting the pencil on the note pad to listen as he went on.

"The guy has a strange face, yet it's honest and trusting . . ."

"Right," she agreed.

". . . His only flaw is that he has devious plans to keep me occupied all afternoon because he thinks I'm awfully cute."

80

Jilly knew her face was turning as red as her sweater as his words echoed in her ears. *He thinks I'm cute!*

He leaned against the open door, obviously enjoying her embarrassment. *"As a matter of fact, you may never see me again. Best regards, your daughter."* He offered his arm. "Well, that's taken care of. Let's go."

Jilly ignored his outstretched elbow, and balanced the note pad on her bent knee, reading out loud as she wrote, *"Dear Mom and Dad. Be right back. Jilly."* She glanced up at him. "My Journalism teacher says not to write more than you want your reader to know."

Leaving the note by the phone, she grabbed a jacket which matched her jeans, and locked the front door.

As he escorted her down the sidewalk, a feeling of caution overwhelmed her thrill of being with him. Jilly suddenly felt as if she were playing a part in an old movie—the kind where the bad guy pretends to like the innocent young girl, only to pry important secrets out of her, then throw her over the nearest cliff.

She'd best be on her guard.

CHAPTER 14

"I don't know your name," Jilly blurted before they'd even pulled away from the curb. She was tired of thinking of him as *the stranger in the blue car.*

"Craig," he said, smiling over at her as he shifted into second gear. "Dancy's Diner all right?"

She nodded. Craig. Now she had a name to attach to his face. It made her realize how little she knew about him. And here she was, going off in a car with this stranger named Craig.

Silence filled the space between them, making her nervous. She had to get the conversation going—and hopefully get some of her questions answered as well.

"So," she began, trying to make her voice sound businesslike, "tell me what this is all about."

"Gee, that's the question I'm supposed to ask you."

Don't let him trap you, Jilly. "You're the one who came to interview me. What are you interviewing me for? Being the most popular girl at Apollo High?" She'd meant it as a joke, to throw him off, but it came out sounding sarcastic, as if she didn't have a friend in the whole world.

He chuckled anyway. "So, are you?"

"Well, if this is an actual interview, I guess I can tell you anything I want and you'll have to report it. Right?"

An expression she couldn't read clouded his face. "Right." He was quiet a few moments. "Seriously, Jilly, are you ready to talk about it?" His tone was sympathetic, as if he was trying to shield her from some terrible truth.

The tenderness in Craig's voice surprised her. She dared a glance which he held with his unblinking gaze. "Why are you so interested in covering this . . . this *story* for your newspaper?" Jilly emphasized the word *story* so he'd know that's all it was. A story made up by Russell Talley. "I mean," she added, "I'm a reporter for Apollo High's newspaper, and I don't get so in—"

"I know you are."

"You do?"

"Yeah. I did a little research, and when I found out you were taking Journalism, I looked for your name in some past issues of the *Apogee*. Our Journalism teacher makes us read and evaluate your school's newspaper so we can keep up with our competition."

"You read my stories?" *Well? Did he like them or not?*

"I was impressed." He slowed the car in the middle of a block while a group of young children dashed into the street, chasing a runaway skateboard. "Especially by the story about building the bell tower in your school's courtyard."

"Yeah?"

"It had everything: Human interest, tight writing, interviews with past alumni. The work of a real pro."

"Thanks." Jilly pretended an interest in the passing scenery. Was he flattering her to make her talk? Or was he being sincere? He *seemed* sincere. "I got an A+ on that assignment," she added, then wondered why she'd told him that.

Craig turned the car into the parking lot behind Dancy's Diner. Jilly opened the door the instant the car stopped, not waiting to see if he would open it for her. This was business, she reminded herself.

They walked around the building, hurrying because a brisk wind had kicked up. Stepping into the diner, they were met with warmth, the smell of fresh-baked pastries, and the hustle and bustle of business.

Craig led her to an isolated booth so they could talk in private, she assumed. The hunger she'd felt earlier had turned into a nervous knot in her stomach. Nothing on the menu appealed to her. Except chocolate pie. Chocolate pie always appealed to her.

Craig ordered two bacon burgers, fries, onion rings, and the local favorite, a Big Apple juice.

He raised his eyebrows at her order. "That's all you want?"

She shrugged. "I could live on chocolate pie."

"Ah, ha!" Craig pretended to open a notebook and write. "A scoop for the newspaper: *Girl Survives on Nothing but Chocolate Pie.*" He looked her up and down, then added: *"And Does So Beautifully."*

She laughed. He was fun to talk to—if only he didn't make her so incredibly nervous.

He pretended to close the invisible notebook and return it to his pocket. "Well, Ms. Milford, how long are we going to keep avoiding the real reason we're here?"

"We can't eat until the waiter brings the food."

He laughed. "Very clever. That's not what I meant."

Jilly was pleased she could make *him* laugh for a change.

His smile faded into the intense look he'd given her in the car. "Why do you refuse to talk about it?"

She was quiet. What was she supposed to say? If she acknowledged that there was an *it,* she would be confirming Russell's story.

He scooted his elbows across the table, leaning toward her. "Russ will go ahead with his story whether you talk or not. In the name of accuracy, Jilly, you really should speak up."

His face, with its endearing freckles, was inches from hers. Jilly was having trouble keeping her mind on his words. "So how do you know Russell is telling the truth?" *That's good, Jilly. Keep talking in circles. Don't commit yourself to anything.*

"You haven't told me otherwise."

"What has he said?"

"He claims there've been several poltergeist sightings

84

in the area of your backyard. And he's making out like it's *his* big discovery. He said he asked for your help, but you refused, so he wants to expose the phenomenon himself and take all the credit for it. He's calling it the Milford ghost."

Jilly laughed at the irony. Jilly's ghost was now the Milford ghost.

Craig leaned back while the waiter served their lunch. Taking a bite of an onion ring, he cocked his head at her. "By the way, I think Russell likes you."

She cringed at the thought as she remembered her self-fulfilling formula for attraction: $J/A = N + J + W$ . . . Attraction to Jilly equals nerds plus jerks plus weirdos.

Scooping meringue into her mouth, she let it melt on her tongue. Something else was still confusing her. "Are you and Russell friends?"

"Not exactly. The only reason he called me is because I write feature stories for the newspaper at his former school—where, I might add, Russell was not exactly a popular person. He's always been considered a little weird."

"No kidding."

Craig paused to sample his burger. "It seems so important to him that his name be mentioned at least every three lines in the story. I think he's in it for the glory. Or to show the kids who taunted him at Massapequa High that he's a big shot now. Who knows what his motives are?"

The chocolate pie was not soothing the knot in Jilly's stomach. Craig's words made it worse. All Russell wanted was his name in the paper and his picture on TV. He didn't care whose secrets he exposed.

Craig pointed a french fry at her. "You obviously agree that Russ is onto something important, or you wouldn't be so upset. You looked as if you wanted to murder the TV cameraman the other day."

He watched her face as if he was waiting for a subtle expression to give her away. "If Russell's story is a hoax,

85

all you have to do is remain quiet and let Russ dig his own grave, so to speak.''

He continued to stare at her as if that might make her give in and spill the whole tale. "But Russell's story isn't a hoax, is it?''

Jilly tried to think of a way she could change the subject.

His eyes never left her face. "You're definitely hiding something. I can tell. And it's something you've known about for a long, long time because you've lived in that house all your life.''

Jilly fanned herself with a napkin, wondering how it had gotten so warm in the diner all of a sudden. "Well, you certainly know an awful lot about me, don't you?''

"It's my job.''

She squirmed in the booth, pulling off her jacket. The more accurate Craig's assumptions became, the more uncomfortable she felt. "Craig, I can't tell you, because . . .'' She paused. ". . . Because I don't trust you.'' There, she'd said it.

He looked surprised. "How can you not trust a guy who buys you chocolate pie for lunch?''

Jilly tried not to laugh. Why did he have to be so darn cute? She focused on the people in the booth behind Craig. "I don't trust you because you're in league with Russell and I don't trust Russell. Both of you want to expose my . . . my secret to the media. It would ruin everything.''

"Ruin everything,'' he repeated. "Now why would reporting a poltergeist sighting ruin everything in this young lady's life? The plot thickens.''

He leaned across the table to whisper. "Are you a ghost, too?''

It was hard to maintain the serious look she'd been giving him.

Craig took hold of her hand. "You *feel* like a real girl.'' He squeezed her hand tighter, then released it. "Yep, you definitely feel like a real girl.''

Business, Jilly. Don't let him influence you with sweet

talk. She leveled her eyes at him, trying to forget how nice her hand had felt in his. "You're going to write this story whether I tell you anything or not, aren't you?" A small part of her heart begged him to say no.

He held her gaze a long time. "The journalist in me says this is one hot story. A story that needs to be told. Especially now that you've got my curiosity cranked up. But the rest of me is tempted to back off for your sake. I don't want to hurt you, or make you any angrier than you already are. However, I'm not sure I can back off now that I've seen—"

All the warmth that had surrounded her as they talked evaporated, sending chills through her. She flashed back to the image of Russell climbing out of Craig's car, carrying the large envelope. "The letters," she finished for him. "You've seen the letters."

"Well, why did you give the letters to Russ in the first place? I mean, the answer to this whole mystery might be right there in the suicide note."

Jilly's anger toward Russell flared once more. "I didn't *give* the letters to Russell. He *stole* them."

"He did?" Craig held his Coke in mid air, waiting for her to confirm the comment.

"Yes. He conned my dad into letting him into our toolshed, where . . ." She stopped. "Now I've told you too much."

The second part of Craig's remark sank in, sending chills cascading through her once more. "What did you say about a suicide note?" *Had Molly killed herself over the loss of her husband? Or had it been Caleb's note?*

"I'm really confused." He set his Coke down. "I thought you'd read all the letters. That's what Russ said."

"No. I'd just discovered them myself yesterday. I've read only a few—ones Russell hasn't seen."

"Oh, so there are more?"

She nodded as a sense of urgency overcame her. "Tell me about the suicide note."

"The note was written by someone name Calvin, I think."

"Caleb."

"Yeah, Caleb. It was addressed to a Molly, but it sounded as if she had died years before."

"Molly had died?" His words made Jilly's heart numb. "Was the note dated?"

"Yeah, um. It was March, 1950 something. 1956, I think."

Jilly did some quick calculations in her head. Samuel died in 1931. What had happened to Molly and Caleb during the next twenty-five years? If the ghost was Caleb, he must have been a lot older than Molly. Or at least the ghost appeared as an old man.

"So, Russ lied to me," Craig said, placing money on top of the check. "The plot thickens even more."

Jilly added her share of the money. After all, it wasn't a date. It was a business lunch.

Grabbing her jacket, she waited until they'd left the restaurant and were back in the car before asking the next question. "Are you going to write the story or not?"

"I have a major decision to make first." He steered the car into the traffic. "Should I believe Russ's version of the story? Or do I trust that you have a mighty darn good reason for keeping this all a secret?"

Jilly held her breath. He'd known Russell a lot longer than he'd known her. How did he know she wasn't the one who was lying?

He gave her a sympathetic smile as he touched her arm. "I'm beginning to wonder who's side I'm really on—yours or Russell's."

Jilly remained quiet during the ride home. Why did it matter to her so much that Craig choose her story over Russell's?

Because Mr. McGregor mattered to her, that's why.

And, her mind added, so does Craig.

CHAPTER 15

Jilly huddled in the dark on her window seat. She was determined to stay there until Mr. McGregor made an appearance. She'd wait all night if she had to.

Cold, she moved across the room to pull the comforter from her bed. Wrapping it around herself, she settled back into her place by the window, hugging Pokie, her stuffed kitten, and watching.

What was she watching for? Was she expecting Mr. McGregor to give her some kind of a sign? Why would he? In fifteen years he'd never once acknowledged her presence. Besides, he didn't appear every single night, so this might be a royal waste of time.

Jilly cuddled the kitten inside the quilt, trying to snap the pieces of the mystery together as though it was a jigsaw puzzle. Suppose Mr. McGregor *was* the ghost of Caleb Hart. Why was he compelled to return to the Milford's backyard year after year, decade after decade? A list of reasons formed in her mind:

1. To retrieve his notes and letters.
2. To be near Molly's home.
3. To take care of unfinished business as the groundskeeper.

Jilly shivered as she remembered the suicide note. Why hadn't she asked Craig what the note had said? Had Caleb killed himself over his love for Molly? Had he killed himself in the Milford's backyard? Mentally, she added to her list:

4. The ghost is compelled to return to the site of his death.

Something must have happened between Caleb and Molly during the years after Samuel's death. Had she married him? Had she jilted him? Had she died before him, as Craig had implied?

Not knowing the answers was driving her crazy.

Poor Caleb.

Poor Jilly.

She shivered again. Would Craig ever come back to see her? If he went ahead with the story, she'd have to refuse to speak to him out of respect for Mr. McGregor. It was a matter of honor. After all, she'd known Mr. McGregor a lot longer than she'd known Craig.

But Craig is real, Jilly. Mr. McGregor is not. He's part of the past. Craig is definitely part of the here and now. How can you be more loyal to a dead person than you are to someone who's very much alive?

Jilly couldn't answer the question she'd asked herself. She tried not to think about Craig—or her future. What did she have to look forward to?

Russell was about to expose her lifelong secret. Jonathan Nichols was falling for her best friend. She was falling for Craig, who was probably interested in her only because of her secret. And she was moving to Florida. Maybe moving away wasn't such a bad idea after all.

Why couldn't Craig be a jerk like Russell Talley? Then it'd be easy to oppose him. She sighed. Just the thought of Craig smiling at her from across the table at the diner warmed her more than the comforter.

Jonathan Nichols came to mind. She'd hardly given him a second thought since Craig had driven his blue car into her life. Craig was so much easier to talk to, and he didn't make her feel invisible the way Jonathan did.

Jilly heard a muffled ring. The phone? At this hour?

Her parents had already gone to bed. Leaping to her feet, she moved across the bedroom and down the curved stairway, trailing the comforter behind like a queen's robe.

It was Amanda.

"Jilly? I hope I didn't wake your parents. Can you talk?"

"Ama-a-anda. What time is it?"

"It's a little past midnight. Did I wake you?"

"No, I was waiting for my date to show up."

"What?"

"Forget it. What's wrong?"

"Nothing's wrong. Everything's perfect. Kevin just brought me home."

Jilly slid to the floor, wrapping the comforter around her. "Tell me all about it," she said, sounding a little like her own mother.

"Jil, I hope I didn't make you mad leaving the library with Kevin. You know how much I like him."

"It was fine. Honest." And she meant it. If Kevin hadn't distracted Amanda, Jilly wouldn't have been home when Craig came calling.

"Kevin told me he still feels the same about me as he did over Thanksgiving break, but he was uncomfortable with how fast our relationship was moving."

"Ah, a guy with depth."

"Be serious, Jilly, he was. He told me he'd meant what he said to me that night in the alley behind 7-Eleven, but he worried that I thought he was rushing me. So he asked if we could start over, and go a little slower—which is fine with me."

"You still haven't explained Traci Wooster."

"It turns out they've been friends all their lives. They tell each other everything. He was actually asking Traci for advice on what to do about me."

"Then why has Traci acted so snooty? Why didn't she tell you Kevin likes you?"

"I think she likes to be seen hanging out with him. I don't think Traci minded for one minute that we thought she and Kevin were going out together."

"Well, all's well that ends well."

"Are you okay? You sound as if I'm boring you."

"I'm just counting all the hearts that will break when you and Kevin are seen together."

"Like whose?"

"Andy Spinner's. Jonathan Nichols."

"Jilly, they're just friends." She paused. "Speaking of Jonathan, have you talked to him lately?"

"How can I talk to him when he's following *you* around?" Jilly bit her tongue. Why had she said that? It made her sound like a whining kid, jealous over a toy.

"Jilly, when you like somebody, you've got to let him know. You can't pine away in silence and expect him to assume you're interested. Speak up. Monday, I want you to walk into Journalism and sit right next to Jonathan."

"That'll be easy if I'm with you."

"No, I'll sit somewhere else."

Jilly leaned her head against the wall. She was falling asleep. Jonathan's face and Craig's face swirled through her mind. Suddenly she could care less about sitting next to Jonathan Nichols.

But she was afraid to tell Amanda about Craig. The same thing would happen. Once Craig laid eyes on her best friend, it would be good-bye Jilly, hello Amanda. She decided to keep Craig her own *heart's secret*.

Saying goodnight, she stumbled up the stairs to bed, forgoing her plan to wait for Mr. McGregor. But she couldn't resist one quick look out the window. The yard seemed quiet tonight, bathed in the light of a half moon.

The light threw a shadow across her window frame, catching Jilly's eye. Two tiny hearts, barely touching, had been carved into the frame. She knew they'd been there for years, but now she'd like to think she knew what they meant: Caleb's symbol for the love he felt for Molly. Two hearts touching, never joined.

There was only one way to find out if they were ever joined in marriage. The answer was hidden in the library. She had the date of the suicide note. Hopefully it would contain the missing pieces of her jigsaw puzzle.

Jilly climbed into bed, willing the day's events to stop tumbling through her mind. The library was closed on Sundays, so she'd have to wait another day to satisfy her curiosity.

She only hoped the parts of the puzzle came together for her before they did for Russell Talley.

CHAPTER 16

At school, everyone was talking about the Winter Carnival coming up on Saturday night. Each school club was sponsoring a booth, and it seemed as if half the students in every class had gotten permission to go to the girls' gym to work on their club's booth.

Last year as a freshman, Jilly's date for the Carnival had been Amanda. At first they'd had fun circling the perimeter of the gym, checking out all the booths. They'd tossed coins into Coke bottles, fished for penny prizes, and posed for caricature drawings.

Then they'd come to the kissing booth. Jilly'd never forget that one as long as she lived.

A bunch of junior guys were hanging around the booth, trying to decide whether or not they should pay a dollar to kiss a girl who was disguised as an Arabian princess. In other words, they couldn't see who they'd be kissing because only her eyes were showing. Ms. Shipley, the club's sponsor was trying to get the guys to lay down their dollars for a kiss to support the Young Authors' Club.

While the guys tried to make up their minds, they spotted Amanda and said they'd lay down their dollars for a chance to kiss her. Ms. Shipley had grabbed Amanda, initiated her into the club on the spot, and talked her into stepping behind the booth.

The club made fifteen dollars in fifteen minutes, only what the junior guys didn't know was that Amanda had chickened out while she was supposed to be changing into the Arabian princess costume.

Ms. Shipley had put the same girl in the front of the booth, called her Amanda, and started collecting money. Amanda had hidden until the guys moved on to another booth.

Jilly had thought the whole thing was hilarious, but Amanda hated all those guys thinking they'd kissed her when they hadn't. Kevin Dobbins still held the honor of being first. Jilly wondered who *her* first would be, and hoped she didn't have long to wait. She also wondered how long Caleb had waited for his first kiss with Molly—if there'd been one at all.

Sighing over her mushy daydreams, she settled into her second period typing class. Would she ever get used to Amanda attracting all the attention when the two of them were together?

She was doing her best to concentrate on today's typing lesson. The clicking of thirty typewriters usually lulled her to sleep every morning, but today her mind was intent on trying to solve the mystery of the Milford ghost.

After typing *You are cordially invited to attend a reception honoring Dr. Barry Quebec* five of the twenty times she was supposed to type it, Jilly began to replace Dr. Barry Quebec's name with others: Samuel Harrigan, Caleb Hart, Molly Harrigan Hart—Jilly hoped that had been her name before she'd died—Amanda Parks, Russell Talley, Craig. . . .

Suddenly she realized she didn't know Craig's last name. Maybe she could locate one of Massapequa High's newspapers and look for his byline. Or simply ask him, if she ever got the chance. She still had his phone number, but not enough nerve to dial it.

Jilly remembered one of the stories she'd made up about Mr. McGregor's imaginary grandson named Craig

McGregor. Wouldn't it be eerie if Craig's last name was McGregor?

When the bell rang, Jilly scrunched her practice papers into a tight ball before trashing them. She didn't want anyone to wonder why she'd been typing Russell Talley's name.

A few minutes later she stepped into Journalism, her eyes searching out Amanda. Amanda's table was already filled, so she obviously hadn't saved Jilly a seat.

Amanda motioned for her to pick the table closest to the window. Jilly was confused for a moment, then remembered her friend's plan to seat her and Jonathan Nichols together. *"When you like somebody, you've got to let him know,"* Amanda had said. *"You can't pine away in silence and expect him to assume you're interested."*

The table closest to the window was usually Jonathan's first choice. She made her way toward it.

Jilly was glad she'd forgotten about Amanda's plan, or she would've been a nervous wreck all morning. This way she didn't have time to get hyper because Jonathan Nichols was heading straight for her table right now.

"Hi," he said, setting his books next to hers.

"Hi." Jilly noticed his eyes immediately traveled to Amanda's table.

Jonathan turned a chair around and straddled it as Mr. Kortman began class by handing out a test. Test day was not a good day to get to know the person next to you.

"Hey," he began as they waited for copies of the test. "Aren't you friends with Amanda Parks?"

"Yes." *Here it comes,* Jilly thought.

"Is she going with anyone?" He paused as Mr. Kortman leaned between them to dump a pile of tests onto the table. "Like, is she going to the Carnival with anyone?"

Jilly reached for a test, trying to act as if she were chatting about the weather with an old friend. "Amanda might be going with someone," she answered, thinking about Kevin Dobbins.

"So is he taking her to the Carnival?" he repeated.

"Shhhhh," whispered Li Sing from across the table.

"I don't know." Jilly kept her voice even. "Why don't you ask her?"

"Well, I—"

"We're taking a test here," she snapped, interrupting him. "Do you mind?" The last thing she wanted was for Mr. Kortman to give her an *F* if he thought she was cheating.

"Are you always this testy at test time?" Jonathan was actually smiling at her.

She smiled back. "Sorry." She bent her head over the test to avoid further conversation.

Jilly tried to concentrate on the first question, but inside she was shaking. Why did it bother her that Jonathan wanted to ask Amanda to the Winter Carnival? It doesn't matter, she told herself. Jonathan likes Amanda. Amanda likes Kevin. And Jilly likes . . . She'd started to say *Jonathan*, but in her heart she said *Craig*.

Jilly likes Craig, she said again to herself. *Jilly and Craig.* She liked the way it sounded.

Only it's not going to happen, Jilly, because he doesn't like you. Not the same way you like him. He's only interested in the Milford Ghost. And now that you refuse to talk about it, he has no reason to see you again.

Jilly was still staring at question number one of the test. She shook her head to clear it. She had to get through this test. Then she had to get through the rest of the day.

The missing clues she needed to solve the mystery of the Milford ghost might be at the library right now, waiting for her to find them.

CHAPTER 17

Jilly waited by Amanda's locker after school. All she could think about was rushing to the library to figure out the rest of the mystery.

The day had been excruciatingly long, and now Amanda was making it longer by asking her to wait.

After Journalism, Jonathan had grabbed Amanda's attention, so Jilly had gone to lunch alone. Amanda never showed up in the cafeteria at all. Jilly assumed she'd spent the lunch hour with Jonathan.

She leaned her head against Amanda's locker. How many guys does one girl need? Jilly asked her invisible friend. Regardless, she refused to feel jealous or be angry at Amanda.

Finally Amanda dashed up—alone. "Thanks for waiting," she said, catching her breath. She dialed the combination lock while juggling her books. "I've been dying to talk to you all day to find out how it went."

"How *what* went?"

"You and Jonathan. Did you talk to him during Journalism?"

Jilly was puzzled. "Not as much as you did."

"What do you mean?"

"Well, you left with him after class." Jilly waved at a passing group even though she didn't know any of them. She wanted to show Amanda she wasn't interested in anything Jonathan might have said to her.

"We just spoke for a second. I thought that you—"

"You didn't go to lunch with him?"

"No. I ran into Andy Spinner and he needed some help with the decorations on the Computer Club's Carnival booth." Amanda pulled on her jacket, then slammed the locker door. She gave the dial on the lock a twirl, then scooped her books off the floor.

Jilly made no move to help her. She did feel angry now, angry at herself. She'd spent the entire afternoon believing that Amanda and Jonathan had shared lunch when they really hadn't. "So what did *you* and Jonathan talk about?" She kicked herself for being unable to stifle her curiosity.

Amanda fumbled with her armload as they moved down the hall. "Who, me?" She acted as if she were stalling for time. "Oh, nothing. Just 'Hi, how are you?'—that sort of thing."

She was hiding something. Jilly could tell. They'd been friends too long for her not to be able to read Amanda's face. Jonathan had asked Amanda to the Carnival and Amanda didn't want her to know.

"The question is," Amanda said, "what did *you* and Jonathan talk about?"

Jilly took a deep breath and smiled back at her friend. She didn't feel angry anymore. Amanda was simply trying to protect her. "Oh, just 'Hi, how are you?,'—that sort of thing," she said, mimicking her friend's voice.

Amanda wrinkled her nose. "Oh well, with the test and all, it wasn't a good day to visit with anyone."

Jilly pushed the heavy front door of the school open, anxious to change the subject. "I'll walk you to your house, then I'm going on to the library."

"Oh, can I go with you? I need to look up Argentina for History."

Jilly turned her face into the wind. Tiny flakes of snow stung her cheeks. She hadn't counted on Amanda going to the library with her. Jilly was becoming possessive with the secret lives of the people whose stories were slowly unfolding before her.

"Jil? Hello?" Amanda leaned over to see Jilly's face. "If you'd rather I didn't go with you, it's—"

"No. I'm just being weird." Jilly reached to take some of Amanda's load, feeling guilty for not helping her friend earlier. "I discovered some new information, and I'm a little preoccupied. I think today is the day I will find out why I have a ghost in my backyard."

"Really?"

Jilly sighed. "I guess I'm trying to prepare myself before I get to the library."

"What's happened?"

"Caleb killed himself."

Amanda gasped. Her eyes doubled in size. "How do you know?"

"He left a suicide note addressed to Molly."

"The letters! You got the letters back from Russell."

"No. I haven't seen the actual note. I just heard about it."

"From Russell?"

"No." Why was it so hard for Jilly to tell Amanda about Craig? *Because the same thing that happened with Jonathan will happen with Craig, that's why.*

She sighed again, pulling her hood up to block the wind. "Remember the stranger in the blue car?"

"Yeah."

"I had lunch with him on Saturday." Jilly glanced at Amanda. Her eyes were even bigger. "His name is Craig."

"Craig McGregor?"

Jilly chuckled, surprised her friend had remembered. "No. I thought the same thing."

They laughed together, making Jilly glad she'd confided in Amanda. She'd have to stop blaming her for being so attractive. Underneath it all, Amanda was still her best friend. They related the same way they had since they were seven years old. Why did she keep thinking Amanda was different now, just because she'd blossomed so much on the outside?

They arrived at the Parkses' house, dumped their books in Amanda's room, then changed into heavier clothes because of the snow.

"I'll go tell my parents we'll be at the library until dinner," Jilly said, not wanting to wait while Amanda applied more mascara and blusher.

Jilly walked into the new addition of the house, inhaling the scent of fresh lumber. The workers had gotten the roof on before the storm had begun. Most of the walls were up, so she could no longer step between the boards into another room. Wires stuck out of holes in the walls here and there as an electrician installed new fixtures and switch plates. Jilly was amazed at how fast the apartment had taken shape.

Mrs. Parks appeared, wearing sawdust in her hair.

Jilly laughed, helping her brush out the sawdust. "Dad puts everybody to work. I know. I've hammered a few nails myself."

"I'm so pleased with how fast they're progressing. My folks have sold their house, and it looks as though we can get them moved in here before Christmas."

"That's great." Jilly peered around a wall. "Where are my parents?"

"Oh, the darndest thing happened today. Your dad's beeper started beeping every five minutes with people calling and wanting him to do some remodeling on their homes. He couldn't figure it out, but he and your mom are running around giving estimates to those who called."

Jilly was puzzled for a moment. Then she remembered the ad she'd run in the *Apogee* for Milford Construction Company. It never crossed her mind that Dad might actually get work from it. She felt pleased, smil-

101

ing at how confused her parents must be from this windfall of good fortune.

Mrs. Parks drove them to the library since the weather had turned so disagreeable. Jilly's excitement mounted as the car grew closer and closer to their destination.

She almost wanted the car to slow down. For fifteen years she'd harbored the secret of *Jilly's ghost*, and in a few minutes she'd be discovering the truth.

Ever since she'd learned Caleb had killed himself, Jilly had known he was Mr. McGregor. Something deep inside her heart told her it was true.

After Caleb killed himself, his spirit was compelled to return to this world for reasons Jilly might never know.

Suddenly it came to her that Mr. McGregor had been appearing in her backyard long before she was even born. The suicide note was dated 1956. The ghost had been haunting the Milford's backyard for almost forty years, and Jilly had been around less than half that time.

She remembered the string of owners who'd lived in the house after Caleb died. Had any of them seen Mr. McGregor? Was he the reason the house had stood empty for twelve years?

Mr. Kortman's voice sounded inside her head as the car stopped in front of the library. *"Every story in a newspaper begins by answering the questions who, what, when, where, and why,"* he'd told them.

Jilly knew the *who, what, when,* and *where* of her mystery. In a few minutes, she hoped to find out the *why*.

CHAPTER 18

"Thanks, Mrs. Parks!" Jilly jumped from the car and raced up the steps of the library.

"Wait for me," Amanda called, running after her.

Taking an elevator to the basement, Amanda found an unused microfilm viewer while Jilly asked the lady at the desk for film of the newspapers from March, 1956. The lady disappeared into the back room.

Jilly paced back and forth, unable to stand still from anticipation.

In a few moments, the lady returned. "Is there anything else I can get for you?" she asked. "Those copies of the microfilm are checked out right now."

"Oh," Jilly replied, disappointed. She started to turn from the desk when it hit her. There was only one person in the world who would be interested in the March, 1956, issue of the newspaper. Russell Talley.

"Amanda," Jilly hissed, stepping back to the viewer. "He's here."

"Who's here?"

"Russell Talley."

"Where?" Amanda's hair bounced against her shoulders as her head flipped in one direction, then the other. "I want to see what he looks like."

"I don't know *where* he is. I just know he's here. Someone has already checked out the papers I need. It *has* to be Russell. Come on, let's find him."

Jilly led Amanda in a circle around the room until she

spotted Russell. Motioning for her friend to stay behind, Jilly stepped up to confront him.

All she needed now, to complicate things further, was for Russell to fall in love with Amanda like every other guy seemed to be doing. Actually it might be the answer to all Jilly's problems. She smiled at the thought of Russell chasing after Amanda.

"You!" she snapped at Russell's back, making him jump.

He rose, looking surprised, then leaned against the viewer, blocking her vision. "Some pretty interesting stuff here," he said, pointing his thumb in the direction of the screen.

Jilly was dying to shove him out of the way so she could read the news story. Instead, she gave him a disgusted look. "You stole my letters," she said in a low voice. "I want them back."

As Russell opened his mouth to answer, Jilly placed two fingers in the middle of his chest, giving him a shove. "I want them back *now*," she demanded.

Pulling her hand away, she took a deep breath to stop her heart from pounding. Her aggressiveness surprised her as much as it seemed to be surprising Russell.

He crossed his arms and grinned at her, crinkling the skin around his scar. He didn't seem half as threatening to her here in the library in broad daylight as he had when he'd stopped her on the dark street.

"I told you I'd figure this out—with or without your help." His hand moved behind him as he clicked off the light on the viewer. "Although I never dreamed the truth would be *this* good. It's going to make a great story."

Jilly narrowed her eyes at him. "Why are you doing this to me?"

Her words startled him. "I'm not doing anything to *you*. I'm simply doing what needs to be done."

"What for?"

"For science."

"For science *fiction*, you mean."

Jilly didn't remember ever feeling this angry with any-one in her entire life. She wanted to shake Russell until he stopped being so obstinate. "I-want-my-letters-back," she said through clenched teeth.

"I'll give them back," Russell answered. "On one condition."

"What condition?"

He turned away. "If you want them back you have to do something."

"Tell me what it is and I'll let you know."

"Tell me you'll do it first—or no letters."

"Russell, all I have to do is call the police and tell them you stole something from me."

"Ah, that would be terrific." He smoothed the hair on his upper lip, not quite full enough to be called a mustache. "Go ahead and call the police. That will give *Newsday* the evidence they've been demanding before they'll believe me. They think I faked the letters."

Russell had her right where he wanted her. She had no choice. "Okay, okay. Give me the letters. I'll do whatever you want."

"Great." He pulled a manila envelope from a grocery sack and handed it to her. Then he clicked on the viewer and pulled out the chair, motioning for her to sit. "In addition to the letters, I think you'll enjoy this little ar-ticle in the newspaper. Dated March 11, 1956. Molly's forty-second birthday—had she lived."

Jilly grasped the letters and stared at the screen's ban-ner headline: *Suicide ends fifteen-year vigil for local man.* But before Jilly could settle in at the viewer and read more, she needed to complete her unfinished busi-ness with Russell.

"So what do I have to do?"

"Go to the Winter Carnival with me on Saturday night."

She stared at him, knowing he was waiting for a reaction. She didn't want to give him the pleasure of watching her cringe.

But he surprised Jilly by giving her a soft look and touching her shoulder with one hand. "Let's not argue about this anymore. You'll forget it after it's all over. We'll have fun together at the Carnival, you'll see."

He was serious. Jilly could tell by the way he was looking at her. He really wanted to date her!

"We started off on the wrong foot," Russell continued, "but I promise to turn it all around—after the story breaks." He gave her a salute. "Few meteors and friendly life forms." With that, he was gone.

Jilly resisted the immediate urge to dive into the news story before her. She motioned for Amanda to join her instead.

Amanda scooted another chair in front of the viewer and sat. "He's just like I pictured him. What did he say?"

"He's going ahead with the story."

Amanda groaned.

Jilly was quiet for a moment. "You know, maybe I should go along with Russell."

"Go along with him? Are you crazy?"

"Well, the media coverage would be hard to take, but it might be the best thing I could do for Mr. McGregor."

"For Caleb." Amanda said, correcting her.

"I know it's Caleb, but I'll always think of him as Mr. McGregor." Jilly swiveled in her chair to face Amanda. "Do you remember when you asked me if I should find out about having the ghost's spirit put to rest?"

Amanda nodded.

"If I let Russell have his way, that's how this whole thing will end. The media will demand that someone be called in to bring an end to the poltergeist sightings.

Then Caleb's ghost can rest for eternity instead of wandering around my backyard."

Amanda gave her an *I-told-you-so* look. "If you'd written your article for the *Apogee* on Mr. McGregor instead of your dad, this might be resolved by now. Without Russell's interference."

"Wait a minute." Jilly scooted her chair closer and whispered. "I've got an idea that's even better than going along with Russell *or* writing about Mr. McGregor." She glanced around to see if anyone was listening, then leaned next to Amanda's ear. "Why don't we ask *Caleb* what he wants and let *him* decide."

Amanda looked at Jilly the way *she* looked at Russell after he said something stupid. "You're being weird again, Jil. How do you propose to *ask* Caleb?"

"A séance."

Amanda shivered visibly in spite of the overheated room. "No. I don't think anyone should mess around with stuff like that. Trying to call up spirits from another world might be dangerous."

"I don't mean we should actually *do* it." The more Jilly thought about the idea, the more excited she became. "I mean, we can make someone *think* we're doing it."

Amanda caught on. "Oh, you mean *fake* a séance? For Russell's sake?"

Jilly nodded. "Brilliant idea, isn't it?"

Amanda's eyes sparked the way they did when she was about to have a burst of enthusiasm. "We could pretend we're having a real séance, get someone to hide nearby, and say something scary to warn Russell away."

They both started talking at once, until the librarian shushed them, so they pretended to concentrate on the viewer screen.

"When should we do it?" Amanda whispered.

"How about Saturday night since I'm going to the Carnival with Russell."

"You're *what?*"

Jilly explained Russell's demand to Amanda. Even though going to the carnival was the last thing on this planet Jilly wanted to do, it would help them pull off a fake séance.

She was relieved she didn't have to go along with Russell after all. She'd simply scare him so badly he'd forget he ever saw the Milford ghost.

Jilly was almost too excited to read the newspaper article on the viewer screen, but it confirmed what she already knew. She had to get Russell off Caleb's track.

According to the newspaper account, Molly and Caleb were to be married on Christmas Eve, 1941, ten years after Samuel's death. Just reading that part of the story thrilled Jilly, knowing that the two had finally acknowledged their love for each other. She was twenty-seven; he was thirty-five.

Jilly wondered about the lapse of ten years. She figured it'd either taken Molly that long to get over Samuel's death, or it'd taken that long for the bashful Caleb finally to tell Molly he was in love with her.

Sometime after their engagement was announced, but before the wedding, Molly had gone into the backyard in the middle of a sudden thunderstorm to make sure Caleb's boat was secured to the mooring. She'd slipped, bumped her head, then fallen into the canal. Caleb had not been there to rescue her, so she drowned.

Jilly brushed a sleeve over her cheek to stop the flow of tears as she read the article. Amanda sniffled softly beside her. *"According to friends, Mr. Hart moved into the Harrigan house and stayed for fifteen years after Molly's death, constantly blaming himself for the tragedy because he hadn't been there to pull his fiancée from the canal,"* she read aloud. *"He took his own life on his betrothed's birthday. Mr. Hart was fifty.*

"Friends of the deceased say Mr. Hart died in the same manner as the one who'd gone before him, drowning

108

himself in the canal behind the Harrigan house. There was no suicide note.

"Ah, but there *was* a suicide note," Jilly whispered, laying her hand on the envelope full of letters. "Only it was addressed to Molly, no one else."

"And no eyes have seen it until now," Amanda added in a solemn voice. "Shall we read it? I mean, this is pretty personal stuff."

"Russell and Craig have seen it," Jilly said. "If they can read it, we can too."

She glanced around at the cold stone walls of the library basement. "But not here, not now. Let's go home. I need to be in my own house, in my own room, before I read the rest of Caleb's letters."

She gave Amanda a sad look. "And before I read Caleb's very last words to Molly."

CHAPTER 19

The girls half walked, half ran through the falling snow, heading down a dark street toward Jilly's house instead of Amanda's so they could read the letters without having to answer a lot of questions. They didn't have much time, since their parents were expecting them for dinner at the Parkses' house.

The sight of the blue car sitting in front of her house gave Jilly mixed emotions. She was thrilled at the prospect of seeing Craig again, but now there was no way to avoid him meeting Amanda. The fact that Jilly was red-faced from the cold with hair matted from the wet snow also dampened the thrill of Craig seeing her.

He opened the car door as they approached. Jilly heard Amanda mumble her approval as Craig's tall form unfolded itself from the car. Jilly's insides immediately knotted.

Craig rushed toward her, flipping his jacket hood over his head to block the snow. "Jilly, I need to talk to you." He grabbed her arm. "We can talk in the car since you're not allowed to have visitors when no one's home." He gave Amanda a polite nod.

Jilly stopped next to his car and waited while he opened the door. "Craig, it's silly to freeze out here when we can go inside. You're not exactly a stranger anymore, and my parents don't have to know."

He held the car door open for her. "I'd rather your

friend waited inside while we stay out here. I need to talk to you alone."

Jilly's heart soared. He hadn't been bowled over by Amanda's looks on first sight after all. *He wants Amanda to disappear so he can be alone with me!*

Confidence surged through her. "Oh, excuse me," she said, turning toward Amanda. "Craig, this is my friend, Amanda Parks. She knows about this whole thing, so it's okay to talk about it in front of her." Jilly wished Amanda would quit staring at Craig.

He seemed uncomfortable. "Nice to meet you," he said, raising a hand in greeting. "But at the risk of being rude, I'd still like to talk to Jilly alone for a minute. Would you mind waiting in the house?"

"Not at all." Amanda beamed at him.

How come wet hair and a red face made her look even prettier?

"Key, Jilly?"

Jilly pulled the key from her pocket and handed it to her friend, thankful that Amanda hadn't argued about being left out. "Thanks. We'll be through in a few minutes."

Amanda smiled at her. "No problem, take your time. I'll call my mom and tell her we'll be late for dinner."

Amanda ran toward the house while Jilly stepped into Craig's car. She twisted the rear view mirror her way to assess the damage to her face and hair before Craig could get around to his side, but it was getting dark—too dark to see her reflection. Good, she thought, it'll be too dark for Craig to see, too.

"So, what's this all about?" Jilly asked as Craig settled into the driver's seat, pulling off his hood. "The story will be on tonight's news, so you came over to warn me, right?" She tried to keep the tone of her voice light.

"No," Craig answered, starting the car and flipping

111

on the heat. "I've had a change of heart." He watched for her reaction.

"Why? Why would you care about people who lived over forty years ago?"

"I don't care about them." He reached for one of her hands, warming it between his. "But I do care about you."

Jilly stared at the large hands enfolding hers. Such a simple gesture touched her more than anything else he could have done. "You do?"

"Yes. I haven't been able to think about anything else all week except you and this incredible secret of yours. And I realized if I went ahead with the story, you would hate me and you'd never speak to me again."

He put his fingers under her chin and raised her face to his. "I don't know whether or not you have a boyfriend, but if not, I'd like to apply for the job."

Jilly laughed, looking away in embarrassment. "Then you're not after me to learn my secret?"

"Is that what you think?" He leaned his head back against the seat. "That's funny. I've been using the infamous Milford ghost story all this time as an excuse to keep seeing you."

"You have?"

"Yeah. Well, I must admit, I was curious about the story in the beginning, but when I had to make a choice between the ghost and you, well . . ." He touched her nose with one finger, grinning at her. "And if you don't believe me, I promise never to mention the ghost again."

"You mean it?"

"I mean it."

"What about Russell?"

"What about him?"

"You'll be letting him down."

Craig shrugged his shoulders. "He's gone overboard with this whole thing. To him, the story isn't as important as it is to see his name splashed across the newspaper. I've already told him I'm backing out because I believe the story is all in his mind." He glanced at her. "Even though your actions have convinced me that Russ's story is true."

"You must have talked to Russell before he found the article at the library."

He raised his eyebrows in question. Jilly knew she was trying to bait him, just to see if she really was more important to him than the story. "Russell found the account of Caleb's suicide from a 1956 newspaper."

Jilly's heart froze in suspense. Would Craig take the bait?

He leaned toward her, pulling her hands to his chest. "Then let Russell worry about it. I'm not going to lose your friendship over it."

He *did* care more about her than the story.

"Friends?" He was so close she could smell his after-shave.

"Friends," she repeated, staring frantically at his freckles, trying to remember what Amanda had said about closing your eyes when you suspect a guy might be thinking about kissing you. When was it that you were supposed to close them?

She blinked a couple of times, trying to decide. In the meantime, Craig kissed her. Right there in front of the old house on Atwater Place. Her very first kiss.

Had her eyes been closed? She couldn't remember now. All she could remember was Craig's warm lips against hers.

Her heart wasn't frozen anymore. She felt as warm as if it was the middle of May.

He kissed her again, soft and slow, then touched his hand to the side of her face. "I think you're pretty," he whispered.

She wasn't going to question his judgment and have him comparing her to Amanda, so she simply said, "Thank you."

Jilly hated to break the spell, but she was making Amanda wait, as well as their parents. And Caleb's letters were waiting to be read. "I need to go," she whispered. "But thank you for respecting my privacy."

He nodded. "Can I drive you wherever you're going?"

"That'd be great," she said, even though she knew it meant bringing him and Amanda together again. She could tell by the way Craig was looking at her that she didn't need to worry about any competition right now. "I'll go get Amanda."

Craig walked her to the house, holding her hand tightly. Amanda swung the door open the instant they stepped onto the porch, making Jilly suspect her friend had been watching them out the living room window the whole time.

"I made hot chocolate," she said, acting like a little mother. "Come warm yourself, then I need to get home." She shot Jilly a look that said her mom wasn't too happy about their delay.

"Craig offered to drive us." Jilly realized she was still grasping his hand. Letting go, she slipped off her jacket and hat, ruffled her hair into place, and followed the other two to the kitchen.

The phone rang.

Amanda jumped to grab it, putting her hand over the speaker to whisper to Jilly, "Russell called a few minutes ago, and I told him you weren't here. It's probably him again." She put the phone to her ear and said hello. A strange expression crossed her face as she handed the phone to Jilly.

Jilly had nothing to say to Russell Talley, now or ever. "Hello?"

"Hello, Jilly? This is Jonathan Nichols."

Jilly's eyes darted to Amanda, who shrugged her shoulders in surprise. "Yes, Jonathan?"

Craig lifted his mug of hot chocolate, then stopped to

114

watch her. Why had she said Jonathan's name out loud? Craig might get the wrong idea.

Jilly turned to one side, leaning against the counter. On second thought, what was wrong with Craig thinking other guys were interested in her? It couldn't hurt.

"I'm calling to ask if you'll go to the Winter Carnival with me on Saturday night."

A million thoughts tumbled through Jilly's mind. She was sure Jonathan had asked Amanda first. Had Amanda put him up to this?

Guilt piled up on her. Amanda knew she liked Jonathan. Her friend was honestly trying to get them together. But now Craig had complicated things—nicely so. And Russell had, too.

Jilly glanced at Craig. He was trying to pretend he wasn't listening to her, but he was. The thought that he cared about her made all the terrible things that had happened since Russell moved in next door seem worth the agony.

"Jilly? Are you there?" Jonathan's voice made him sound much younger over the phone than he was.

"Yes, um, I can't go to the Carnival with you. I have another date." Jilly tried to lower her voice so Craig wouldn't hear, but he did. She hated referring to Russell as her date, but the deal was made, and at least it would solve her Jonathan Nichols problem.

"You do?" Jonathan sounded surprised. *"Well, some other time, maybe."* Now he sounded relieved.

Jilly hung up the phone and leaned over a chair, grabbing her mug of hot chocolate, acting as if guys called her every night. "Thanks, Amanda." She smiled at her friend and raised the mug. Jilly knew that Amanda knew she was thanking her for trying to fix things up between her and Jonathan, not for the hot chocolate.

Craig emptied his mug and pushed back from the table. "I should have believed you when you told me you

115

were the most popular girl at Apollo High." He chuckled, but an injured look settled upon his face.

Jilly shot an embarrassed glance at Amanda, then touched Craig's arm. "It's nothing. He's just a guy from one of my classes. And my date for Saturday night is none other than Russell Talley."

"You're going out with *him?*" Craig acted shocked. "Boy, you're full of surprises. I thought you had a healthy dislike for Russ Talley."

Jilly choked on her drink, coughing. "You don't understand. Russell is *making* me go to the Carnival with him. It was the only way I could get my letters back."

"That jerk." Craig raised to his feet and started toward the back door. "I'm gonna go have a little talk with Talley."

"Wait." Jilly pulled him back into his chair, then told him—without any reservations—about their plan to stage a fake séance to scare Russell away from his quest to expose the Milford ghost. "If I'm Russell's date on Saturday night, it'll be easier for us to get him here at midnight for our little show."

Craig laughed as they laid out their plans. "You guys are pretty smart. Can I volunteer to be Caleb's voice? I'll practice talking like an old man."

Jilly was pleased. She hadn't thought about Craig teaming up with them against Russell. "That'd be great. But remember, Caleb's not *real* old. About fiftyish."

"No problem," Craig said in his best fiftyish voice.

Jilly and Amanda laughed at him. Jilly loved the way Craig was giving all his attention to her instead of Amanda. She was so used to the tables being turned. And Amanda seemed just as thrilled that Craig's attention was aimed at Jilly.

After they finished their hot chocolate, Jilly hustled everyone out to the blue car, knowing her parents would launch an all-out search party if they didn't show up at Amanda's house soon.

Sitting in between Craig and Amanda on the trip to the Parkses' house made Jilly feel happier than she had in months. By next week, Russell would be off her back, Caleb's secret would be safe, and she would have Craig all to herself.

Jilly snuggled close to him as he drove with one arm around her shoulder. He kept smiling down at her. She never thought she'd be thankful to Russell Talley for anything, but now she had him to thank for bringing Craig into her life.

Her instant of happiness began to melt, like the snowflakes hitting the windshield. She'd forgotten about the impending move to Florida.

Why couldn't time stop long enough for her to get everything in her life perfect before tumbling her into change once more?

CHAPTER 20

Jilly fluffed the pillows around herself, burrowing in against the cold before opening the manila envelope. A tiny reading light attached to the headboard on her bed cast an eerie glow across the colorful quilt, leaving the corners of her room shadowed in darkness.

It seemed an appropriate setting for going back in time to unravel the mysteries of someone else's life. The tragedy of losing one's love seemed so incredibly sad to Jilly. She tried not to relate it to her own life.

At least Caleb had had years with Molly. Was she to have only a matter of weeks with Craig? After her dad had announced at dinner tonight that Christmas break might be a good time to visit Florida, Jilly's mind had been in a fog. Dad was thrilled over the business her ad had brought in, but all the remodeling projects sounded short-term—not enough business to keep them in New York. Dad had decided to run a similar ad for the Long Island newspaper, and she was eager to get started on it. The sooner it ran in the paper, the better.

As much as she enjoyed spending evenings at Amanda's house, tonight had been agony. She thought her parents would never finish their work so they could come home. Not only was she dying to read the rest of the letters, but she wanted time alone to think about Craig, remembering everything he did and everything he said. Memories to think about in Florida.

Ah, well, she'd think about her own problems later.

Right now she had someone else's problems to worry over. Someone who'd died decades ago.

Opening the manila envelope, Jilly spread out the ancient, yellowed papers, trying not to wrinkle them. She hated the thought that Russell had seen them before she had.

Tears slid down Jilly's cheeks as she read the notes, poems, and letters. Twenty-five years of Caleb's melancholy life unfolded before her. She assumed by his words that he was excruciatingly shy. Too shy to tell Molly he was in love with her. Jilly could certainly relate to his shyness.

She gathered from the letters that Molly had grieved for years after Samuel's death, choosing to live alone in the house Samuel had built for her as his bride. Comfort and support came from Molly's friend and groundskeeper, Caleb Hart, who stayed on, watching over her. Caleb lived in a nearby house, but spent his days with Molly.

His letters spoke of long hours tending Molly's garden together, talking in the gazebo, and taking his small boat down the canal to the Great South Bay, or across the bay to Jones Beach for picnics.

It sounded so romantic, Jilly thought, searching through the letters until she found the one that explained how Molly went from being Caleb's *heart's secret* to his fiancée:

My Dearest Molly,
My heart is close to bursting with news of your love for me. How could one man be so lucky? I never thought you could ever return an ounce of the feelings I have for you. But to hear how you've waited for me to confess my love! Please forgive me for every moment I've made you wait. I was so afraid if you knew, you'd banish me from your presence, and I'd never gaze upon your lovely face again. But we will wait no longer. This December you will be my bride, my own Christmas angel, my heart's secret nevermore.

Yours,
Caleb

119

Jilly added another wadded Kleenex to the pile beside her bed. Why had Caleb been so dense? Why hadn't he married Molly years before, then filled the Atwater house with lots of children? Molly had to knock him over the head with the fact that she returned his love. Two people in love, too shy to tell each other.

Jilly reassembled the letters and returned them to the envelope, setting aside the suicide note and a yellowed newspaper clipping to read last. She vowed never to avoid telling anyone she loved him. Life was too short.

The letters had stopped abruptly. There were no more until Caleb's suicide note. Jilly assumed the letters had stopped with Molly's death.

Opening the newspaper clipping shocked Jilly's heart. A faded picture of Molly stared back at her from under the word *Obituaries,* dated September 30, 1941. Molly looked much the same as she had in her wedding picture, although ten years had elapsed.

The story was a longer version of the one she'd read this afternoon at the library. The last sentence read: *"Molly Harrigan and Caleb Hart were to be married on December 24th."*

Jilly wasn't sure whether her heart could take any more sadness. She refolded the clipping and returned it to the envelope, then laid her hand on Caleb's suicide note as a wave of dread surged over her.

Jilly, it happened fifty years ago, why is it making you so upset?

While considering the question, she dozed, light still on, hand resting upon the note.

Sometime later, the sound of a train whistle roused her. Sighing, she clicked off the reading light and climbed out of bed, carrying the note to the window seat.

In the cold darkness Jilly watched, waiting for a shadowed movement or a light in the toolshed. The whiteness of the snow covering the ground might mask any movement tonight.

Suddenly the thought of Mr. McGregor returning to the toolshed, only to find his letters missing, sent chills slithering up Jilly's spine. Did he know? Somehow she didn't think Mr. McGregor would be angry. If he knew about her at all, he'd know she was trying to protect him.

If anything, he'd be angry with Russell Talley. Maybe he would haunt Russell, making him wish his family had never moved to Atwater Place.

Jilly liked the idea of Mr. McGregor haunting Russell. She'd have to tell Craig, so he could make that clear when he spoke as Caleb's voice at the séance. She pictured Craig in his old man's voice saying, *"Ruuussellll Taaalleeeey, I wiiill hauuunt yoooou forrreverrr if yoooou dooon't leeeeave meee aaa-looone."*

Jilly smiled in spite of her disappointment at not seeing Mr. McGregor tonight. On second thought, she was glad not to see him. How could she watch him while reading his suicide note at the same time?

With trembling hands, Jilly unfolded the note. She held it close to the window, catching the whiteness from the ground and sky to light it for her.

It was short, simply saying:

My Dearest Molly,
*Fifteen years ago, I made the biggest mistake of my life. I was not here when you needed me most of all. You will never know this, but I was off arranging a surprise for you for our wedding. I was scripting a sign, a new name for my old canal boat: **The Molly Hart**. I love that name, but now it will never be yours.*

My life has been nothing since the night of your death. I choose to join you, suffering the same pain

121

*you suffered, entering the next world where I know
you'll be waiting for me as I have waited for you, my
heart's secret nevermore.*

*Always and Forever,
Your Caleb*

The note was sadder than she'd wanted it to be. Returning to bed, she put the letters in a safe place under her mattress, then treated herself to a deep, heart wrenching sobbing session.

Had Molly truly been waiting for Caleb when he'd entered the next world? If so, why did he keep returning to this world?

Amanda's comment that ghosts were people who've left something in their lives unresolved came back to her. Even death must not have been enough to relieve Caleb's guilt for not saving Molly.

Jilly felt a calmness come over her after she couldn't cry anymore. "Mr. McGregor," she whispered into the darkness. "What can I do to help you? Are you still blaming yourself for Molly's death? Is that what's keeping you from her after all these years?"

Jilly willed herself to stop thinking about the star-crossed lovers because the sadness was more than she could bear. She cocooned the quilt around her, the way she used to do when she was thirteen.

Oh, to be thirteen again. She wished she could return to the time when having a ghost in her backyard was comforting instead of disturbing, when best friends weren't a threat, when business was booming for her parents, when her neighbors were nice instead of weird, and when she could have cared less whether or not a guy liked her.

On second thought, she wouldn't change the last part of her wish for anything.

CHAPTER 21

"Good morning!" Jilly called, rushing into the kitchen the next day. Her dad was at the counter, peeling an orange. Jilly raised to her toes and kissed him on the cheek. "I love you, Dad," she said.

A look of surprise crossed his face. He put the orange down and gave her a hug. "I love you, too, Jil. Is anything wrong?"

"No." Grabbing a slice of his orange, Jilly left the kitchen and toured the downstairs until she found her mom folding towels in the laundry room. "I love you, Mom," she said, hugging her.

"What's wrong?" Mom asked.

"Nothing's wrong. Why does something have to be wrong for me to tell people I love them?"

Mom's face turned misty. She handed a pile of folded towels to Jilly. "I love you, too." She paused. "You're sure nothing's wrong?"

"Jeez, Mom." Jilly shook her head and laughed, then headed toward the linen closet to put away the towels.

The week continued with more rain and sleet, mixed with snow. Amanda's mom drove the two girls to school every day because of the cold, wet weather.

Everyone at school seemed hyper, both due to the overcast days and the upcoming Carnival on Saturday night. As much as Jilly dreaded going out with Russell, she couldn't wait to stage the fake séance. She only hoped her timing was right, because Russell was up to something. She could tell. His footprints decorated the snow in their backyard every morning. Had he discovered more clues? Something Jilly had missed?

At school Russell was going out of his way to be nice. Normally she never saw him in the course of the day, but now he appeared after every class to chat and walk her down the hall. She had ducked into the restroom a million times this week, trying to get away from him.

Then there was Jonathan. He was certainly aware of her existence now, even if confused by her actions. He'd been watching her all week, as if he was wondering how come she could like him, but not go to the Carnival with him. Jilly wished Amanda hadn't told Jonathan she liked him. Now she felt self-conscious every time he was around.

Kevin Dobbins and Amanda were inseparable all week and had plans to go to the Carnival together.

Everything seemed to be falling into place—except for the move to Florida. Jilly's dad's ad was running in this week's paper. All she could do now was keep her fingers crossed.

The best part of the week was that Craig had called every night. His pretense for calling was to make plans for the Saturday séance, but they ended up talking about everything else in the world, too.

After worrying to Craig about how she was going to explain him to her parents, he asked if he could come over Friday night to meet them and take her to a movie.

By the time Friday arrived, Jilly was sure she'd lost five pounds since she hadn't been able to sit still all week. All she could think about was going out with Craig.

On Friday night, Jilly paced the entire length of the upstairs thirty-four and a half times, waiting to hear the sound of the blue car stopping in front of her house.

It finally came.

After checking her hair for the umpteenth time and wishing it was flowing and kinky like Amanda's, she took a deep breath and hurried down the curved staircase. Craig was below, shaking hands with her dad while his eyes watched her run down the steps.

Mom appeared and Jilly introduced them. That part was easy, but then no one could think of anything to say.

"Well?" Craig asked, opening the door.

Dad helped Jilly with her jacket, then she and Craig were off, getting into the blue car and heading down Atwater.

Craig looked gorgeous. Jilly impulsively started to tell him so, remembering her vow to let others know how she felt about them. But her shyness won.

"You look gorgeous," he said, smiling over at her.

"So do you," she said back to him. *Well, that was certainly easy.*

They sat in the back of the movie theatre going over Saturday night's plans in whispers. Either the movie was dull or they simply had too much to talk about, but neither one of them could keep still during the film. Finally they slipped out and drove to Dancy's Diner for some homemade pie and coffee.

"Are you having fun?" Craig asked, warming her hands in his from across the booth.

"Oh, yes," Jilly answered, never believing she could actually be with someone she liked, who not only liked her back, but was easy to talk to. So much for her formula for attraction. "I'm just a little jumpy about tomorrow night."

"It'll be great." Craig released her hand as the food arrived. "The only bad part of the evening will be sitting home, knowing you're at the carnival with Russ."

"Are you jealous?" she asked, dipping a finger into the meringue on top of her chocolate pie.

"Naw. I only get jealous over guys from Planet Earth."

125

The snow kicked up again, blanketing the streets with a fresh layer, so they didn't linger at the diner. Craig wanted to get her home before the streets became too slick.

He drove to her house slowly, partly because of the storm, and partly—Jilly hoped—to lengthen his time with her. They talked over Saturday's plans one last time in front of her house, then she led Craig through the side gate to the back. He wanted to check out the yard and try the microphone he had stuffed inside his jacket. They planned to hide it before the séance, then use it to convince Russell that Caleb was talking to him.

Craig inspected the gazebo, where the séance would take place. In the morning, Jilly would set up a card table in the middle, covered with a long tablecloth. Hidden underneath the table would be a small amplifier. Craig extended the wires, making sure they were long enough to disappear into the bushes, which is where he'd be hiding with the microphone.

"Perfect," Craig said, rewinding the cord. "Can we store this in the toolshed until tomorrow?"

"Sure." Jilly unlocked the back door to her house and tiptoed inside to get the key ring from the basement stairwell. The television was on so she hoped her parents hadn't heard her come in. Returning to the backyard, she unlocked the shed, stepping aside to let Craig in first.

On a sudden impulse, she knelt to show him where the letters had been hidden. He pulled her to her feet, turning her toward him in the tight quarters.

His arms went around her. They held each other for several long moments, not speaking. Then he bent to kiss her.

Drawing back, Craig studied her face in the dim light coming through the window from the white sky. "Excuse me, aren't you the ghost girl?"

She touched his face with her mitten. "Yes, and I plan to haunt you for a long, long time."

"I hope so," he whispered, kissing her again.

Funny how the temperature in the tool shed could be 900 degrees when it was snowing outside.

They stepped from the shed. Jilly pushed the door closed, locking it, and stuffed the key into her jean pocket. Craig put his arm around her as they walked to the front yard.

"I'm not ready to go in yet," she said. "I'll say goodnight here, then I want to check out the backyard again."

"You're not cold?"

"Not anymore." She smiled up at him, wondering if he knew what she meant.

"I can't wait until tomorrow," he whispered.

"So we can get even with Russell Talley?"

"No. So I can see you again."

One more kiss, and he was off, running toward the blue car. Jilly watched him drive away, then returned to the backyard, not ready to go inside and answer a lot of questions from her parents. She wanted to return to the shed where Craig had held her and kissed her. She wanted to recapture the warm, magical feelings he'd given her.

Unlocking the shed, she stepped inside again, leaning against the workbench, feeling Craig's arms around her once more. Wondering what time it was, she resisted the urge to pull the string above her, turning on the light so she could see her watch. It might draw unwanted attention from her next door neighbor. She pushed the button on her watch instead. Eleven o'clock.

Jilly peeked through the window toward the Talleys' house. It was dark. They must be out tonight, she thought.

Glancing up at the bare bulb, Jilly remembered the time when she was seven years old, and the light blew

127

out. Her dad wasn't in any hurry to replace it. Jilly had worried that Mr. McGregor wouldn't be able to see, so she'd pestered her dad until he helped her change the bulb.

Mr. McGregor. Was he here tonight with her? The thought that he was didn't even frighten her. What did she have to be afraid of?

Stepping from the shed, Jilly locked the door, then walked through the snow to the gazebo. Rain was falling now, turning the snow to slush. She slipped as she stepped into the gazebo, catching herself by the railing.

Pulling off a mitten, Jilly ran her fingers along one of the columns until she felt the double hearts carved there. One for Caleb and one for Molly, his *heart's secret,* barely touching. Now she understood the hearts. Tomorrow she would carve two new ones. One for her and one for Craig, barely touching. Her *heart's secret nevermore.*

Shivering, she stepped off the gazebo and slushed her way to the edge of the canal, slipping twice, but catching herself before she fell.

"What am I doing out here?" she asked the melting sky. "I'll probably catch my death of cold."

But something held her there. It was as if tonight was the last night things would be the same. She couldn't explain the feeling, but it was strong.

Jilly stepped along the edge of the canal, watching the reflection of the rain plopping into the murky water. She remembered the night last week when she'd looked at her reflection and had sensed someone behind her. Would it happen again?

As she leaned over the dark water, her foot slipped. Throwing both hands out to break her fall, they splashed into the water instead. Her head hit the cement wall. She opened her mouth to scream, but water rushed in, choking her.

Jilly felt herself go under. She tried to remember what

128

to do, but there was a terrible pain in her head. Her whole body went numb. She couldn't think. Where was the surface? Why was she going down instead of up?

Kick, she told herself. Her boots were too heavy; they were pulling her down. She tried to shove them off, but her arms tangled in her jacket.

Cold. So cold.

Pain flashed like lightning through her head, making her body tense, then relax. She breathed in water instead of air. Seconds slowed to minutes as a shadowy dream began.

Jilly watched the dream as if she was outside herself. What was she fighting for? She'd forgotten.

Floating, Jilly gave in to the pain. She found it easier to let the darkness of the shadowed dream consume her than to resist.

CHAPTER 22

"Molly . . .

"Molly . . ."

The voice sounded far away to Jilly. It would stop for a while, then come back. Was it Craig's voice? Jilly could see his face, his eyes, his hands reaching out to her. She tried to reach back but he was too far away.

"Jilly."

Her eyes flew open. Whiteness surrounded her. Not the whiteness of snow, but of a hospital room. Her dad bent over her, a worried frown creasing his forehead. She'd never noticed before how old he was starting to look.

"Did you call me Molly?" Each word throbbed a pain inside her head.

"No," he answered, swiveling. "She's awake," he called to someone across the room.

Her mom appeared, along with two nurses, who began checking the electronic equipment circling the bed.

"How do you feel?" Mom asked, brushing hair off her forehead.

Jilly lifted her hand to her head, feeling a bandage. "I'm not sure. What happened?"

"You fell into the canal," her dad answered, watching her face. "We didn't even know that you had come home."

In a rush it came back to her. Craig, the snowy backyard, falling. "Who pulled me out?" she asked in a whisper, trying to lessen the throb when she spoke.

Her parents exchanged glances.

"Who saved me?" she repeated.

"You saved yourself, honey," Dad answered. "Don't you remember? I heard a noise in the yard and found you lying unconscious beside the canal."

All Jilly remembered was going under the water, being cold beyond belief, the numbing confusion, then going to sleep. She knew she'd flailed her arms at first, but hadn't been close enough to the bank to touch it, much less pull herself out. "No," she mumbled, meaning *No, I didn't save myself.*

"Are you having trouble remembering?" Mom asked. Not waiting for an answer, she turned to the nurses. "She's having trouble remembering."

While the nurse explained that some people blank out the details of a tragedy, Jilly ran the scene through in her mind again. There was nothing wrong with her memory. She was positive she hadn't pulled herself from the canal. *That* she would have remembered.

The nurse gave her a shot for pain. Jilly took hold of her mom's arm. "Will you tell Russell I can't go to the Carnival with him tomorrow night?" *See?* She wanted to add. *There's nothing wrong with my memory.*

"Honey, the Carnival was last night."

Jilly was confused.

"This is Sunday afternoon," Mom explained. "You've been unconscious for almost forty-eight hours."

"I have?" A million thoughts sprang into Jilly's mind. The Carnival. The séance. What Russell might have done by now. Craig.

"You get some rest," Dad said, giving her a fatherly pat on the shoulder. "We've been here two days, waiting for you to wake up. We'll go get some rest ourselves and come back tonight."

She kissed them both. "Dad? Any calls from the ad yet?"

He smiled at the nurse. "There's nothing wrong with my daughter's memory. She's still plotting ways to keep me from moving her south." He patted his pocket. "I've got bids in on enough jobs to keep me busy for about three months. Not enough to keep us from moving, but not bad for one week's worth of calls. I decided to postpone the move and keep running the ad to see what happens."

"Oh, Dad, thank you!" Jilly tried to lift her arms for a hug, forgetting she was wired to a battery of machines. "Whoops," she said, letting him hug her.

After they left, Jilly tried to sleep, but something was wrong. Dad's words came back to her. *You saved yourself.* No she didn't. Someone else saved her life. But who? Craig had gone, Russell hadn't been home, and it obviously hadn't been one of her parents. Who had pulled her from the canal?

The feeling which had troubled her Friday night returned to haunt her once more. The feeling that things would never be the same again.

Something had changed. She felt as if her jigsaw puzzle was almost complete now, except for one piece.

Dr. Mary Colleen came in to check on her. Jilly was patient through all the proddings and probings, answering the doctor's questions dutifully.

"You're one lucky young lady," Dr. Colleen said, pausing to make a few notes on a clipboard. "If it hadn't been for that rope, you couldn't have pulled yourself out of the canal before your body temperature dropped below the danger level. I don't know how you had the presence of mind to do it after getting such a nasty blow to your head."

"What rope?" Jilly asked. There were no ropes tied to the mooring anymore.

"The rope used to tie up boats," Dr. Colleen an-

132

swered. "Your dad said no boats had been docked there for decades. He couldn't understand where the rope came from. Figured it was some kids playing along the canal who tied it there."

After the doctor left, Jilly settled back onto her pillow. Even though she didn't understand, it was very clear to her now. She knew who'd saved her.

Mr. McGregor—Caleb.

Caleb had somehow gotten a rope from the toolshed and had pulled her out of the canal.

Caleb had saved her life.

Jilly, you're crazy. Then it came to her. The feeling that something had changed. Caleb—Mr. McGregor was gone. For good. She had sensed it was going to happen on Friday night.

The missing piece of the puzzle snapped into place in her mind. Caleb had been returning to her backyard for forty years, full of remorse for not being there to save Molly from drowning.

It was too late for him to save Molly, but, with Jilly, Caleb had been given another chance. Another chance to go on into the next world, free from his chains in this world.

Free at last to be with Molly.

Caleb Hart, her own Mr. McGregor, had saved her life and was gone forever to find his eternal peace.

A tear fell onto her hand. Jilly wiped her face, not wanting any of the fluttering nurses to see her crying.

Mr. McGregor was gone. She should be happy. She had helped him find his peace and go home to Molly.

Jilly sighed, sliding further under the covers, holding her bandaged head with one hand. She'd be happy tomorrow. Right now she felt miserable.

"Knock, knock" came a familiar voice as Amanda bounced into the room. Behind her came Craig.

Jilly sat up straighter, arranging the covers, and noticing for the first time she was wearing an ugly hospital gown with tiny purple and green flowers on it. She wondered how her hair looked and tried to smooth it as best she could with the bandage in the way.

Amanda noticed her primping. "This is no time to worry about what you look like." Tears filled Amanda's eyes. "I'm so glad you didn't die, Jilly, you scared me so much." Her voice trembled out each word.

Jilly let herself be hugged. "Amanda, I love you," she whispered into her friend's ear.

"I love you, too, and don't you ever go falling into the canal again or I'll murder you." Amanda borrowed some tissues from the bedside stand and blotted her eyes.

The nurses left them alone, with a warning to keep the visit short.

Craig looked uncomfortable, waiting for Amanda to finish blubbering over Jilly. He pulled up a chair and leaned his elbows on the bed close to Jilly, studying her face.

She cringed from the scrutiny. "I've looked better," she said.

"You look terrific." His voice was soft and gentle. "You're alive. I've been kicking myself for two days for leaving you in your yard in the middle of the night during a storm, and not making sure you were safe inside before I left."

For a moment Jilly imagined the same conversation happening between Caleb and Molly—had she lived.

She was touched by Craig's caring and the tender way he was looking at her. "I'm sorry I had to cancel the séance, but—"

"*We* didn't," Amanda said.

"What?"

Craig touched her arm gingerly, acting as if she would break if he pressed too hard. "We went ahead with the séance because we thought you'd still want to scare Russell away."

"You did?" Jilly's eyes went from one to the other. "Did it work?"

"Like a charm," Amanda answered. "Your parents were here at the hospital, so they didn't even know we borrowed your backyard. The only change in plans was that I had to tell Kevin what was going on. He came with me and played Caleb instead of Craig."

"Yeah," Craig added. "We were afraid Russ might recognize my voice. Kevin did a great impersonation of an old man. He told Russ if he didn't stop tailing him, he would have horrible luck for thirty years. Poor Russ was white from panic, just from hearing the unexplained voice. Kevin could have given a weather report or told a joke and it would've scared Russell just as much."

Jilly laughed. The painkiller was working on her head, making it throb a little softer.

Amanda stuck her right hand in front of Jilly's face. A class ring encircled her middle finger.

"From Kevin?"

Amanda nodded. Jilly could tell she was dying to spill the details, but couldn't with Craig there.

The medicine was also beginning to make her drowsy, but she didn't want them to leave. "I can't believe you guys pulled it off," she said. "I'm sorry I wasn't there." She would have given anything to see a petrified Russell Talley.

"We may have pulled it off," Craig said, "but I'm not sure it'll solve your problem. As long as the ghost is there, Russ will be causing trouble, trying to figure it all out."

Jilly knew there was nothing to worry about now. There'd be plenty of time to explain what happened to Craig. Or maybe she'd keep it to herself. He might think she was crazy.

A nurse stepped into the room and tapped her watch, warning them to leave.

"There's only one thing that didn't make sense,"

135

Amanda said. "Kevin claims he didn't say something, but if he didn't, then who did?"

"What was it?"

"He said *'Thank you for keeping . . . something safe.'* " She paused, turning to Craig. "Was it *'for keeping my heart safe'?*"

He shrugged. "I thought it was *'my secret.'* "

Their words echoed in Jilly's ears. She knew exactly what it was. *"Thank you for keeping my heart's secret safe."*

So it was true. The ghost had reached back into this world during the séance to make contact with her. And he wanted her to know it.

The nurse reappeared. Amanda gave Jilly another hug. "Hope you get out of here soon. I miss you." She backed toward the door. "I'll call you later," she said, pointing toward the phone. "There're a *million* things I want to tell you."

Jilly laughed at the urgent winks Amanda was giving her, then waved goodbye, glad that life for Amanda was progressing as normal.

"I gotta leave," Craig said, nodding at the nurse. "I'll call you later, as well, because there're a million things *I* want to tell you, too."

Jilly felt strength surge through her body from Craig's hand. "Thank you," she whispered.

"What for?"

"For believing my side of the story instead of Russell's."

"Well, I was heavily influenced."

"How?"

"You're a lot prettier than Russell is."

Jilly hid her face behind one hand. "Even now?"

He pulled her hand away. "Even now." Rising to his feet, he kissed her on the cheek. "Get well in a hurry. There's a slice of chocolate pie at Dancy's with your name on it."

He threw her another kiss as he headed toward the door.

"Craig?" she called after him. There was one last thing she had to find out.

He stopped and turned. "Yeah?"

"Your last name doesn't happen to be McGregor, does it?" Her heart told her it would be too much of a coincidence, but still time seemed to hover, waiting for his answer.

"No."

"Oh." She sighed. "Well, I didn't think so."

He waved and stepped toward the door.

"Craig?"

"Yeah?"

"What *is* your last name?"

"You're just getting around to asking my last name?"

"I've been preoccupied."

He laughed. "My name's Hart. Craig Hart." With that he was gone.

Jilly clicked off the overhead light and closed her eyes to sleep. Craig Hart. *Come on, Jilly, you can't attribute everything that happens to the ghost's influence.*

Was it the ghost instead of Russell who'd brought Craig into her life? Could Craig be a great great nephew of Caleb's?

Naw, Jilly said to herself. That would be a coincidence you'd only read about in a book.

As for Mr. McGregor, it was time for her to let go and give up her childhood fantasies. She was almost sixteen now, and she had her first boyfriend who thought she was pretty and who liked to kiss her.

"Good-bye Mr. McGregor," Jilly whispered into the pillow. "Go in peace and be with your *heart's secret evermore.*"

But I'm glad for a while you were a ghost.

My ghost.

Jilly's ghost.

DIAN CURTIS REGAN has previously been employed as a North Pole elf, an integrator operator, a Tupperware lady, a waitress, an address label proofreader, a schoolteacher, a cartoonist, a model, a movie extra, and an oscilloscope inspector. She now writes books for young readers from her home in Oklahoma.